Christopher

BLOOD BROTHERHOOD BOOK 4

KATHI S. BARTON

World Castle Publishing, LLC
Pensacola, Florida
Copyright © Kathi S. Barton 2016
Hardback ISBN: 9781629893730
Paperback ISBN: 9781629893747
eBook ISBN: 9781629893754
First Edition World Castle Publishing, LLC, January 25, 2016
http://www.worldcastlepublishing.com

Cover: Karen Fuller
Editor: Eric Johnston
Editor: Maxine Bringenberg

Chapter 1

Christopher sat on the cold concrete and leaned his back against the hard wall behind him. His body temperature had finally leveled out, but not enough that he could go without some sort of fan or other form of cooling agent to keep himself from roasting all the time. He looked over at the woman who sat next to him. She was covered in as much blood and gore as he was. The battle, like most of them, had not been a pretty thing. And they seemed to be getting worse all the time.

Usually he would simply do his job and then go back to his room. He was spending a great deal more time out and about with the rest of the people in the house, but for the most part, he loved being alone. But Chris really enjoyed talking to Vicki…he thought she was a hoot.

"The next time the alarm goes off, I'm going to hunt it down and tear it apart." Chris said nothing as Vicki sat there with her eyes closed and continued. "I swear to you, as soon as this crap is done, I'm out of here and finding a nice warm beach to lay on for about ten years. I'm going to eat ice cream for every meal, and wear a dress with high heels when I fucking want to. Which I might add, I have never wanted to before now; but that's not the point, is it?"

"Do you think it will?" She asked him what he meant without looking in his direction. "End. Do you think this will ever end? Because I have to tell you, it doesn't feel like it on most days."

Of late he'd been feeling like it was the same shit every day. Get up, fight, shower, eat, and then go to bed, only to have to do it all over again the next day. He knew that there were fewer and fewer of the monsters, but they were no less vicious in their pursuit of trying to kill more people. And that was another thing. There were fewer and fewer humans around as well.

"Hector wants us to find some newbies if we can." Chris looked up at Skylar when she spoke, and wondered not for the first time if any part of her body wasn't tatted up. He was pretty inked up himself, but most of his had been there before any of this had gone down. Skylar even had them on her face and neck. But for some reason, he still thought she was beautiful. "There is a new project going on across the way. Who wants to go with me?"

"I will." Chris stood and helped Vicki up as he turned to Skylar to ask her how they were going. Her wings spread out and he backed from her. "I'd rather take a car if it's all the same to you. Nothing against your flying ability, but I would rather just drive."

"And how would that be fun for me?" He nodded and found himself wrapped up in her arms and soaring dizzily into the deep blue of the sky. "Are you getting along any better, Chris? You seem to be less inclined to stay in your room. I'm glad for that. It's fun having you around more."

He wanted to ask her why she cared, but they were currently several hundred feet in the air if he were to piss her off. Which, he supposed, he'd managed to do more often than he liked to think about. But right now, she would more than likely drop him on his head.

"I don't really mind being here. But...." He couldn't put into words how much he hated what he was doing. He was pretty sure that she got it, but he didn't know how to convey it to her. "I was famous once. An entertainer, as you know. Women would throw themselves at me. Panties, bras, sometimes even money. Men too, but that wasn't going to happen. And now look. Not only am I pretty much just a normal person, no one cares much that I was once considered the most sought after male in the world."

"Whine much?" He only winced at her words, still not comfortable enough with the rest of them to be his usual self. His old self would have flashed her his smile, winked at her, and told her that was what made him so irresistible. "Nate and I had a conversation about you the other day. He thinks you're a blowhard. Whatever did you do to him to make him hate you so much?"

"Breathed? I don't know. Now there is a whiny person. He's not coming out of his room for anything, is he?"

Before he could ask her what the two of them had talked about—or actually argued about—they were landing. Chris looked at the malefactors and wondered why someone would do this to humans. He'd heard the stories, but he knew that there had to be something more than that. When they entered the building where a small group of them were, Chris thought that they'd made a mistake about them being here. But then he saw the groups as they walked around like.... Chris turned to Skylar when it occurred to him what he was seeing.

"Have you ever played one of those first person shooter games?" Skylar said that she had played on her phone a few times, but not lately. "Yeah, no cell service. But when you're playing and have to leave the game—I don't know, to take a piss or something—when you return, your guy will be walking straight into a wall, his feet still moving as the monsters or whatever are clawing at him or blowing him to bits with their guns. That's what they look like, a game version of sleep walking."

They stood watching the dozen or so of the monsters do just that...walk into a wall and continue moving their feet toward some unknown place, but staying where they were. One of the men, walking around rather into things, had a large gash in his head where his head kept hitting the fire alarm signage just where his head was. Over and over the guy would do this until he was dead, Chris supposed.

Chris moved toward them just as a creature moved from between two of the pillars holding up the other floors. Neither he nor Skylar moved as the thing, just as clumsy and stupid as the malefactors, moved about the room. Chris thought he might have been an adherent at one time, but now he'd lost some of his color and he was no longer in charge. As he knocked a desk over and then tripped several times when he tried to stand and keep moving, neither Chris nor Skylar moved to help him. As soon as he got to whatever he'd been working his way toward, he stopped and turned, almost as if he were a solider on a march and he was at the end of his area.

"Why didn't he trip into the desk before? I mean, it's obvious that he's been doing this same thing for a while. Why hadn't he tripped up before?"

Chris started to tell Skylar that he didn't know when it occurred to him. "He's making a circle. See? Judging by the footsteps that he's made in the dirt on the floor, the circle's getting smaller with each of his trips around the room. It looks like he started out on the perimeter, then tightened his circle an inch or so with each pass — or I guess square, because of the room — more each time." They both watched him and the people in the room as a second thing occurred to Chris. "Do you hear that? That small hum, like there is power somewhere?"

As they spread out, looking for the power grid like those they'd been destroying every time they heard one, Chris moved to the second floor and paused. He'd learned a great deal over the last couple of weeks working with these people, and one of the things was always to be thinking outside the box. But the one in front of him, as big as a nice sized SUV, had him pausing and wondering what sort of shit was about to go down now. The box was addressed to him and Skylar.

Skylar came up behind him and asked him what he was doing. "I don't have a clue, but all I can think about is that movie that had the big lamp leg in it. Remember that movie?"

"Yeah. Christ, I love that movie. We should see if we can find it somewhere while we're out. I bet Remy hasn't ever seen it." Chris said nothing. Remy was one scary mother fucker, and the man seemed to exude strength all over his body. To think of him watching that movie, eating his beloved popcorn, was just too weird. "What should we do?"

The handwriting was old world, the script on it something that he'd seen Remy use when he had to make notes on something. The man would take an hour to write out something that Chris would have just scribbled on a piece of paper. Remy told him that to do something right was to take your time with it. You never knew who was going to look at it. Chris supposed Remy was right, but there were times when he just wanted to take the paper from him and write the note himself. This looked like it might be from Bob, another old world guy.

"You think this is part of the gifts that Bob said would come to us when we needed them?" Again, Chris had no answers and said that to Skylar. "Well, do we open it? Leave it for another day or what? I'm not all that keen on getting my ass kicked by whatever is in that thing, are you?"

The big dragon had left them a letter a while back. Well, not them, but Leo and Jamey. It had said that when they needed it, something would appear. But this thing wasn't addressed to his workmates, but to him and Skylar. He glanced at Skylar when she asked him again if they should open it.

"I don't fucking know. You're in charge." That got him a hard knock to his head that hurt like hell. "I'm all for having enough shit going on. If we open that, and I'm not saying that we should, what's to say that it's not filled with some more of these things that plan to eat our faces off?"

"You are no longer allowed to come with me on these things. You are one freaked out cat." He felt the cat stir along his skin and Skylar smiled at him. "What if there is a gorgeous young woman in there that will satisfy your every desire and then some?"

Chris felt his heart twist up. He wasn't going to find his other half. He'd done that already, and she was now dead. Thanks to him. But before he said something that would get him knocked on his ass this time, he moved toward the huge crate. Whatever was in that thing couldn't be as bad as losing your mate.

There was a note attached to the top of it, and he knew immediately that it was indeed from Bob the dragon. The handwriting couldn't have been from anyone but him. Not that he could read the script there, but he knew it was from him. Pulling one of the bright orange straps off the top of the box, he handed the note to Skylar and put his sword back on his body.

Things had gotten shit weird when he'd gotten here. He'd had tats before, but nothing like he'd gotten the day after arriving. He and Remy had been in the sublevels of the compound, sparring. And when Remy had—he wanted to think it was innocent on his part, but he wasn't sure—but when Remy had put out his hand to help him stand up after being knocked on his ass, the most incredible pain had taken him to the floor again. That was when he discovered the sword at his back and the guns, big ones, on different parts of his body.

The lid, like the crate, was made of wood. And when it slid off the opening, he moved back while the dust settled around them. It occurred to him, too late, he realized now, that he more than likely should have thought this through a little better.

"Nothing?" He wasn't sure and told Skylar to stay back while he checked. "In the event you didn't notice, I'm as strong as you are. And I can fly out of the way if the thing really does try and eat our faces off."

"Yeah, I noticed all that. But if this shit is going to kill one of us, I'd rather it was me so you can go back and warn the others. I really don't care to have to explain to Remy that I let you fucking get your ass handed to you." She took a step back and told him she was sorry. Chris turned to look at the crate again, thinking he needed to get a grip on his temper. "So am I. But please, just stay back out of the way in case there is something in here that has bloodletting on his mind."

Moving closer to the crate, he looked inside. It was dark, which he supposed he should have counted on. But that was all he could see. Just an inky blackness that suddenly made him think of his heart. As he peered harder inside, his cat, never very friendly to him anyway, snarled at him.

"Do you suppose he knows something that you don't?" Very possible, and he told Skylar that. "I see. And do you normally ignore him when he might be trying to tell you something? Or do you feel, like most men, that you know more than your counterpart?"

It was right on the tip of his tongue to tell her to fuck off. He knew, somewhere in the back of his mind, that not only would it piss her off more than she seemed to be right now, but that it would also get him in trouble with Remy. The man was very protective of his mate. Just as he was thinking fuck it and started to tell her off, a sound...a low keening sound...came from the depths of the darkness of the crate.

~~~

Kate watched the couple as they stood by the crate. It had arrived...well, arrived might have been the wrong term for how it had gotten there, but it had appeared sometime in the last twenty minutes. The thing, like the people downstairs, had just sort of come into the building like it had every right to be there.

She'd been hanging out, sort of living here, for a month now when she couldn't get back to her place before it was too dark out. It was quiet, and the things on the lower levels never ventured up here when they came around. But today this crate had arrived, and then the creatures below, almost at the same time.

The sound that had emitted from the box had been there before too. Kate had even gone close enough to the crate to see if someone, a person, was inside, but all she heard was rumblings and an occasional bump on the wall. She had wondered what it was, but not enough to open it and see. The man opening the box made her want to hide deeper in the shadows, just on the off chance that it wasn't going to be a nice wedding gift for the two of them, and instead something that would most assuredly kill all of them. Kate moved back further when she saw the man stiffen. Then the sides of the crate fell away.

"What the fuck?" Kate moved out of the shadows again—not close enough that she thought they could see her just yet, but she, too, was curious about the contents of the box—when the woman yelled and stepped back. What she wasn't prepared for was the man shifting into a big black cat.

He seemed to know she was there even before Kate could think that the cat might come at her. As she turned to run, the cat, bigger than any that Kate had seen in the zoos when they had existed, came after her. Kate knew about paranormals and other shifters being big, but this cat was much larger than even them.

She knew in that moment that he was a different kind of shifter, and she didn't want him close enough to touch her. But by then, it was too late. When she was pinned to the floor, his big body over hers, she was terrified that he was going to hurt her. He couldn't kill her, she knew, but pain was pain.

She looked up when a shadow moved over her face. The woman was there, and she looked amused for some reason. When she knelt beside her, Kate saw that like the man, she was tatted well beyond what she thought of as a social norm.

"I'm Skylar. This lug on you is Chris. And you would be?" Kate said nothing. "Ah, the strong silent type. Okay, I get it. But he's not going to let you up until we get some answers or whatever is in that box comes out and tears us a new ass. But hey, it's completely fine with me."

Kate could have gladly gotten up and murdered her. But Skylar only stared at her as she stood over her. The man, the cat really, growled low and Kate looked at him. Even as a cat, he had the most incredible eyes.

They weren't the dark color that she'd seen on cats. Shifters usually had the same color of eyes as their other bodies did. Browns usually, an occasional green or blue if the shifter had been turned. But Chris had blue eyes. Just as blue as the oceans she'd seen over her lifetime. And as she watched them, Kate was sure that she could see large animals, some of them as ancient as she was, moving in them. With a shake of her head, she tried to think how to get out of this mess.

"We have movement."

Kate was suddenly free. The cat, Chris, had moved off her, but not away. He was close enough that she could touch him, his dark fur touching her arm that he was closest to. Her fingers burned to run all over him for some reason. But when the noise started again, she looked over at the crate as the couple was doing.

A bundle of cloth inside the crate moved. She supposed it might have been moving all along, but since she'd been on the floor, the building's walls below them could have caved in and she'd not know it. Well, she would, but that wasn't the point right now. When it moved again, the cloth falling away, the first thing she thought of was that it was a tiny paw. The second was that whatever it was, it wasn't alone in the blanket that fell open.

Then it occurred to her what it was. Well, what they were. Puppies. There were about ten or so of them, and they came bouncing out of the cloth on the floor and toward them like they'd been ordered to do so. As soon as they were near her, Kate couldn't help it…she pulled one of the little creatures to her face and it licked her.

"Chris, I'd very much like for you to be a man again." Kate wondered at the tense sound of Skylar's voice, but was too excited to have the wiggly puppies coming to sit all over her legs. She could see now there were eleven of them. Eleven roly poly little balls of fur. "Remy is coming. He said to stand down until he and the others get here."

Stand down? They were puppies for heavens sakes. But when one of them went to stand by Skylar, she moved away from it like the thing was going to tear at her leg. Kate wondered if the woman had ever had a dog in her life. Laughing, she called the pup back to her and loved on him to sooth his hurt feelings.

"Why would they be in such a big box?" They both looked at her as she stood up. "The box came this morning and I wondered about it, but as it wasn't addressed to me, I didn't bother opening it."

"Who are you?" Kate wasn't going to answer that. She of all people knew enough about magic, and there was little doubt in her head that these two were covered in it, and that names were kept close. "I'd really like for you to tell me what the hell you have to do with all this."

"I had nothing to do with them. Are you afraid of them? Because I'm pretty sure that you can pretty much squash them if they look vicious to you or something." Kate reached down and picked up the one currently sitting on her foot. "They do look like they might rip your throat out, don't they? Do you suppose they have something more than just their milk teeth? Perhaps they have five inch long incisors that will tear at you too. I know, you're afraid of their claws. Let me see…oh yeah, I can see how these little things could tear into your flesh while they chew at your throat."

"I don't like you very much." Kate shrugged at Skylar, not really carrying if she did or didn't. There were a lot of people that didn't like her, and right now, having this woman not liking her might be a blessing. Kate put the dog down and headed for the stairs.

"Where the hell do you think you're going?"

"Home." She didn't stop as she made her way down the stairs. They'd try to follow her, but she doubted very much they'd be able to for long. Kate had powers of her own, and she wasn't the kind of person that many would fuck with.

As soon as she was on the lower level of the building, she paused when she looked at the creatures. She heard rather than saw the big cat come up behind her. He didn't move to knock her down, but watched her as she kept an eye on the creatures.

"There is something wrong with them. They're not like the others, are they?" He said nothing, but moved to stand closer to her. Kate moved away and he stayed where he was. "I don't mean the fact that they've been changed into something, but there is something else here. Like they've had their brains sucked out for the most part and they aren't able to function. Just look at them. Someone has hurt them other than just being the creatures they were."

The man that was walking into the wall fell over. His head had a large hole in it, and a part of his brain was still hanging on the sign that had at one time proclaimed there was a fire extinguisher below it. It had long ago been taken by someone, she guessed.

Moving to the door, avoiding the creatures, she was just going out the door when a huge man landed in front of her. Remy, she'd bet, and she started to back up enough so that he'd not touch her. But she fell backward, the cat behind her getting caught up in her feet, and she went down. And for the second time that day, he landed on top of her.

"Get off me, you moron." The cat didn't move, but Remy laughed down at them both. "You think this is funny? I don't. Call off your animal and let me go. I have places to be."

The movement out of the corner of her eye startled her. Just as the big bird—or whatever the fuck it was…the thing—came swooping down, she reached her hand up and grabbed Remy by the leg. Pulling it out from under him, Kate lifted her other hand and blasted the creature just as it put out his claws to no doubt grab up and kill someone. More than likely her.

No one moved as the big bird like thing screamed in pain as it died. His feathers, if that was what they were, burned brightly, the gaping hole in his chest bled badly, and she knew from experience that it wouldn't last that much longer. Kate looked at Remy when the big cat finally moved off her.

"You know what that is?" She told him she'd seen them around as she stood up. "And you have some sort of power that makes it so you can kill them. What are you? Who are you?"

"There'll be one more. They travel in pairs." The sky darkened over her head and they all looked up when she did. "That's his mate, I think. The male attacks first. Not sure why…he's the weaker of the two. Then the female will come in and take whatever is left after he…he kills his prey. Usually humans. They don't touch the other creatures."

"Malefactors." She asked him what that was. "The creatures. The ones that are walking around now. These are a little…I'd say slower, but I'm not sure that's all it is. What do you know about them?"

Skylar spoke before Kate could. "She said she knows nothing. But they're being drained again. And here, this is what Bob sent us."

The little puppies were now in a box that Skylar handed to Remy. They scrambled out and were all over him when Kate decided that she'd had enough cuteness for one day, but before she could move to take off, the big cat stood in front of her.

"I don't want to have to hurt you." The cat yawned and Remy laughed behind her. Kate turned to him then. "Tell him to leave me alone. I saved your ass. I don't owe you anything."

"No. You do not, and I thank you for saving me. But for some reason I have a feeling you saved your own butt and not mine. Is that true?" Kate said nothing, but felt her fear of this man double when he stood up. Even having a puppy in his arms did not lessen how much she was afraid of him, nor lessen the fact that she knew that he'd try to kill her and never put the little dog down. "I'd very much like for you to say you'll come back to the compound with us. I have many questions for you."

"No." He nodded, and before she could guess what the hell was going to happen next, she felt powerful arms around her and she was soaring up in the sky. Mother fuck, Skylar had her, and she wasn't going to be happy when she figured out what Kate was. "I won't stay there. Wherever there is."

"Maybe, but now that I have your scent, you won't be hard to find again." Kate didn't tell her that it wasn't going to work either, but held on as they made their way across the city. It was different seeing this city with someone carrying you. The only time that Kate had this view was when she was flying herself.

As soon as they landed, Remy and the box of puppies did as well. There were children in the yard, and as soon as the little dogs tumbled out of their temporary home, the children—about a dozen of them—came running. Kids and puppies went together like they were meant to be. As soon as she was let go, Remy took to the sky again to no doubt get Chris. Kate looked at Skylar.

"I won't stay." Skylar nodded and turned to the building. Kate stood where she was, not really feeling the need to chase after the woman and tell her again that she wasn't going to stay. Things were...they weren't out of her hands. She would give them what information they might want about the bird things, but that was all. Nothing else was any of their business.

Chapter 2

Chris tried to not think of the woman. But he knew as surely as she popped in his mind every ten seconds that trying to forget her was like telling himself that he wasn't to breathe. There was something about her that made him crazy. Not to mention that since meeting her, or seeing her in this case, he felt stronger. And that frightened him on so many levels.

"You ready?" Chris looked at Remy when he spoke and realized he had not one clue what he was talking about. He knew that Remy had noticed that Chris had not been paying attention when he laughed at him. "The meeting. With the woman. She's going to tell us what those things were, and a few other things while she's willing to stay. Have you been out this entire time?"

"I was thinking." Remy seemed to be asking him about what without actually saying anything, and Chris felt inclined to explain. He stretch his neck muscles, hearing them pop, and started to pace the floor. "She's a shifter. I'm not sure what she is, but she isn't just a shifter. And not like any I've ever seen."

"Skylar said she touched her but still can't figure out what she is. And there is a block on her mind that she can't breach either. Whatever she is, she's keeping it pretty much to herself. And I think that as soon as we get what we can out of her concerning some of the things we've seen lately, she'll leave. Do you suppose she has something to add to our group?"

Chris waited for Remy to ask about her being his mate, and knew that it was impossible. So when the question came, he was ready with his answer.

"She's dead. My mate died a few years ago, before I came here." Chris knew the exact date, time, and minute that his mate had died. He'd been with her...she'd died in a car accident that had been his fault. "My kind are only given true love one time. I wasted mine long ago."

"You wasted yours? How?" Chris moved to the window that he knew hadn't been in this room before. It occurred to him that the view was wrong. That he was positive that they were nowhere near the ocean. Yet he could see the big liners on the water as if they had a front row seat to them. "Chris, are you sure that this woman isn't your mate? Did you make a mistake the first time?"

"No, there was no mistake. She was...only our mates can carry our child. My wife, Pella, was pregnant when she was killed." Chris didn't bother looking at his friend. He knew that Remy had lost his wife too when she'd been with child, and he didn't want to see the pity or whatever on his face. "I drove us over a mountainside when we were on our way home from a party. We were fighting. Again. She told me to slow down, but I was too...too much me to listen. Her neck was broken and I was thrown from the car. Our child died when there was no one there to help him come into the world."

"I'm sorry." Chris had heard it before. But he knew that Remy was sincere in his words. Only a man who had lost a child would understand how he really felt. "I truly am. But there is something about this woman that bothers you. What is it?"

"I don't know. When I touched her, knocking her to the floor, my first thought was that she was with Benton. Not that she gave us any indication that she was, but it was...the fear factor, I guess, that made me think that. Then, as soon as I looked into her eyes, there was something so calming about her that I felt my cat relax. For the first time in ages. Then it felt as if she looked at him; not at me, but right at my cat." Remy asked him what happened when he didn't continue right away. "There was this connection. Like...I'm not sure. A connection that ran deep. Like she knew all there was to know about me and wasn't really impressed by it. I'm not sure why that thought is there, but you asked."

"Why don't you sit down with her and talk? Maybe she can tell you why you connected." Chris had thought of that and dismissed it. She wouldn't give him any more than she had Remy, and he'd been using his mind control thing on her to no avail. He'd wanted to answer him when Remy had used it on her, and he'd not even been the target. "I don't know how to help you. I suppose you could ask Skylar. She will more than likely know more than we would anyway. She's had the most contact with her, not that there's all that much going on verbally between them. Christ, I've never seen Skylar so frustrated with anyone before."

"Have you ever heard of an elite shifter?" They both turned to Rick when he entered the room. Chris had hoped that Nate would be joining them, but the man stubbornly refused to have much of any kind of contact with them. He was there, and that was about all he could say about the man. "I heard from my friend, Janell. She said that there is a movement that is going on that Benton is behind. She said that he's trying to get others to come here and get beyond our boundaries, and then do something to make it so he could enter here as well. I guess he's figuring that once they're in, they'll be able to invite others in, like it's some sort of human house that we can't enter."

"You mean that's true, about you guys not being able to enter a house unless invited? I thought that was a myth or something." Chris felt stupid the moment the question left his mouth. "I'm sorry. That was rude. And even though I am a fucking bastard most of the time, I didn't mean to pry into your private business."

"It's fine, and true to a point. If a person invites us into their dwelling, be it home or cave, we can go in and be free to do anything and everything to them and their home. Entering a home without an invitation limits us by cutting off our ability to feed from those that live and work there. I have no idea why, but there has to be at least a little permission going down before we can have fun." Rick laughed. "I was kidding, Chris, about the fun part. Believe it or not, we're not all bad people, just that we were painted as monsters long before this shit started to happen."

"Not according to some of the covers I've seen about you guys." Remy asked Chris what he meant. "I heard them called bodice rippers. Or smut. You can call them a lot of names, I guess, but they're read by women all over the world, and they paint vampires as this sex crazed beast that only feeds off helpless women when they're in the middle of this sex orgy."

"Some portray the women as the strong bossy type too. And it's sort of a fun thing in these books to try and tame the woman, when it's the man that usually gets his ass handed to him." When Rick realized what he'd said, they all laughed. "Yes, I've read them. And have found them to be pretty good. There are a few that I've actually wondered if the author was indeed a vampire, but I've never checked to see. But back to my friend. Janell said to expect a few more vamps to come our way too. As well as a man by the name of Tim. Tim, she said, is harmless, but very easy to manipulate."

"And you trust her?" Rick told Remy that he did with his life, and had on occasion. "I see; and we're going to have to trust her as well, I guess. I wish there was a book. I'd just like once to say, yes, I knew that. I read it in our book."

They had all wished that. In fact, young Ruben, Hector's son, was working on a sort of manual now. He called it his summer reading. So far as Chris could tell it was turning into a novel, perhaps even a couple of them the way he was going at it. There were lists of things they could each do, what their tats looked like, and things that happened that only mated couples could do. He'd been photographed so many times by the kid to create a working knowledge of the work on him that he was sure that the kid could point out things on him that Chris wasn't aware of.

As they moved to the gathering room, a large open room that had couches instead of chairs, drapes on the windows instead of blinds, and a long table of the best food in the world set up in the event that things went long and they might need a snack, Chris wondered what was going to happen to this place after they were finished with this assignment. Not just this talk, but with all the malefactors and Benton too.

Everyone was there when the three of them arrived. Chris looked at the woman, who had only spoken to a few people...the kids a lot more, and she played with the puppies. He'd even gotten down on the floor with them and let them romp all over him. He'd been completely surprised when they showed no fear of him smelling like a cat. Bob, in his note, had told them that the puppies, all of them, would be medically beneficial to them in the coming weeks. Chris believed the big dragon was right. He certainly felt better having them around.

Two of the little guys had been given to the daycare center to let the kids play with. Ann had taken one of them to keep her company, she said, and he was now sitting at her feet while the rest had the run of the building. He was wondering who was going to clean up after them when the woman cleared her throat to speak.

When she paused, her head tilted to the right as if she were listening to someone or something, Chris had a sudden thought that she was talking to Benton again. He wasn't sure, but he didn't trust her as yet and figured that was it. He stood up when she looked at him.

"A friend of mine is in need of assistance. I would suggest that we tread lightly where he is concerned. Things are not always as they seem, he said." He nodded, not having a clue what the woman was talking about, but headed for the door. He was both surprised and a little pissed that Rick started out with him and the woman.

"I can handle this, I think." Rick nodded, but didn't pause in his walking with him. "Seriously, just let me handle this."

"The man is my friend as well. I want to go and help him too. You can have your fun with the woman if you want, but after we go to my friend." Chris wanted to ask him if he knew what was going on, but Rick only smiled at him. "You smell of her. Otherwise I'd tell you to sit the fuck back down and I'd handle whatever he's gotten himself into."

They waited while the woman said she'd be back in a few minutes. Several volunteered to go as well, but Remy said that they'd be fine, to call if they needed them. He was glad to know that someone had some confidence in their ability to take care of this.

"Of course I smell like her. You were told that I knocked her down several times. What does she know about this that you and I can't handle?" Rick only laughed, which made Chris think that the man needed his head taken off. "Why won't people just say what you ask them? Every time I ask a question lately, I get laughed at or my question goes unanswered."

"You asked me one question, Chris, one that you know the answer to already. We're going to see what she can do. And I'm up on the rotation with you. That's all." Chris said nothing, not understanding him at all. Not really understanding anyone lately, it seemed. "This woman, I think she walks where few would, does what is least expected of her, and treads on toes that are better left alone. What do you think?"

"I think she's trouble." Rick was still laughing when they got into the large vehicle, with the woman in the back. Chris turned to her. "What are you?"

"Does it matter?" No, he thought as he buckled in. He'd ridden with Rick before and knew the man had a death wish when he was behind the wheel of the car. "I'm a little of everything. Elite shifter for sure, vampire too, but made not born. That's really all you need to know. I go by Kate. You can call me that or continue calling me that woman. Either works for me since I won't be here very long."

He thought about when he was holding her down. She'd looked into his eyes and he had a feeling that she could see him. Really, really see deep inside of him. And that she might know all there was to know about everything that he'd ever done, ever said, and who he had hurt and loved. To be honest, Chris was a little afraid of her. Rick told him that he should be just remembering that the man could read his mind as well.

Why do you say that? Rick just looked at him, then at the road again. *You say that like you really mean it. What do you think you know about her? Or me, for that matter.*

Because, my friend, I believe that she's one scary bitch. And when cornered, I'd stay the fuck out of her way if I were you, even if you're not on the receiving end of it. Chris asked him how he knew. *I don't for sure. But I'd say, just from what I've heard, that there is something more about her than she's letting us see right now. I think that Kate has some very deep secrets that no one will know unless she lets you. And even then, I'm not so sure I'd want to know what she knows about us. I'm a little...I was going to say afraid of her, but it's more than that. I'm terrified of what she might know.*

Chris was still thinking about her when they pulled up in front of the building. He'd been by here several times in the last weeks, mostly to go from one point to another, but today, he looked in the shops and wondered what they were doing there. They weren't damaged. Not a single window was broken out. There was no trash in front of the building, and he thought there might be electric to the place. He knew that they'd not bothered with this end of town as yet. Then he saw him.

"That your friend?" Rick said that it was. But instead of moving toward him, the three stood still. When he moved finally, coming out of the alley between two buildings to the left that they were parked in front of, Chris watched as he shifted from human to bird in breathtaking beauty. As a hawk, the man landed on Rick's shoulder.

"This is Cobb...he wants us to stand here for a few seconds. There is something he wishes for us to see in that building right there." They watched, but Chris found himself paying more attention to the bird than his surroundings. He wondered what he was too. Then Kate spoke to him through a connection that he'd not known was there before.

You cannot see if you do not look. He nodded and grinned. *What is so funny? You do need to know this. And why are you even here if you have no intentions of paying attention to your surroundings?*

I came here because it was my turn to go out. She asked him who made these rules. *Remy and Skylar do. They thought a schedule would keep us in better spirits and rested. How is it you can talk to me?*

I can talk to all lesser beings. Before he could ask her what that meant, she told him to look at the building. "See it?"

The entire building shifted. Not like an earthquake might have caused if there had been a tremor, but like they were watching a movie and the film or whatever had been spliced, and there was too much missing to make it a good flow. Before he could ask what that meant, it did it twice more.

"Three times. It happens three times, and then it stops for precisely thirty-one minutes before it does it again." He looked over at the bird and saw that he was a man again, and Chris wondered who the hell he was. And more importantly, how he was a friend of Rick's and how Kate had known to bring them here. "I set up a timer and a camera, but so far all I've been able to see is a blur on it. I don't think the cameras can pick it up as well as the human eye can."

"What is it, do you suppose?" Chris pulled out his phone and tried to guess how long it had been, and set his timer for five minutes less than he thought thirty-one minutes would be. He looked up when neither of them answered him. "You know."

Cobb shook his head, then nodded. Before he could ask him to explain it, Cobb looked at Kate. He wondered how they knew each other as well.

"It's not a real place. At least I don't think it is." Chris moved closer to the building, close enough to touch it, which he nearly did before Cobb called him away. "It's not real, as I said, and touching it will...it's harmed several people already when they tried to enter this place. Also, you should know that I have been in the back of this building and it looks nothing like this. On that side when you enter, there are empty boxes, clothing that has had better days, and the smell of rotted food. As you can see, this place looks to be freshly painted and well stocked with books. Of all kinds."

"Books?" Chris stepped closer but still didn't touch it. "I don't see books. I see shoes. Displays of shoes on mannequin's feet, as well as boxes of them behind them. I can see into the storefront as well. There is an old fashioned cash register, as well as a jacket hanging on a coat rack. There is dust on the counter, but not any books that I can see."

"I see neither of those. I see women's things, in an array of colors. Sexy things, deep reds and white. Not the sort you'd see in a department store, but the kind one would buy online for your other half." Rick looked at him and smiled. "Perhaps I should show you that site. It's very nice. It might go a long way in getting you to be less stressed all the time."

Chris had no idea what he was talking about, and even if he did, there was no way he was going to comment. But he looked at the building again. This time he saw it too. Lingerie. Scantily dressed mannequins that looked like the woman beside him. It made him think of sex and Kate. Her tangled up, not just in the sheets, but him as well. He could almost taste her dewy sweat from making love all night. Her naked beneath…. Then it hit him.

"It changes to be what we want it to be. I mean, on the inside. The view, it becomes what we think of." He flushed when Rick winked at him again. "Think of food, something that you'd like to have, and it's there. I was thinking I need to get me some new boots, and that's what I saw. You saw books…I'm assuming that you enjoy reading. It's a catch, like a beautiful display in a big store front that is there to bring you in to spend money. Someone wants to lure people into this place."

"And the jump in time? Could it be that its magic is not yet stable, or that it's only a small attempt?" Chris had no idea, but thought that could be it when Kate suggested it. "So, this place, it's an attempt to get unsuspecting people to come in, and then what does it do to them? Change them? Or is there another reason that you can think of as to why someone would put up such an elaborate display of magic?"

"Could it be a portal of some kind? Like a lure to get people to go to wherever Benton is?"

Chris thought that was it. He knew that no one had seen Benton in a few weeks and they had thought he was dead. Hoped it, really. But if this thing was what they were saying, and he had no doubt that it was, Benton or someone like him had to be doing it. But for what?

"Most of the people in the other realm are gone, we thought. Nearly all of them have come here. But do you suppose that there is no one left there? Just the three of them?" Kate asked Rick who they were. "Benton is the creature that has taken it upon himself to kill all mankind. At the orders of Ward and another man by the name of Dolin. We've been wondering what has happened to them since we've not really heard from them in a while. And since the number of malefactors is decreasing more and more each time we go out, we assumed that they were dead. Or something has happened to their equipment used to make them."

"So you think they set this up to make others go to them. To do what?" No one had an answer, but Cobb cleared his throat. "Do you know?"

"I have a guess. Most people, humans that have not been changed, walk by. They look in, see whatever they want, I know now, but ignore it for the most part. I guess...well, since you've set up most of the grocery stores and other places of business, most of what we need is readily available now. But there have been...I would call them engineers. Or something like that." Chris asked him what they did. "Two of the men in lab coats entered a few days ago. I don't know what they might have seen...I was seeing blankets, but I'd not compared my seeing with anyone else. Then just today, three men went in as well. I heard screams and started to enter when I thought of all the other things that have been going on and decided to call for help. I'm glad that I did now."

"Do you suppose that now that all the people who worked in the labs are here, they've decided to see if they can bring some back to do whatever they had been before? That they might need some help getting the labs up and running again?" Chris looked at Rick when he said that made sense. "Well, that's really fucked up. We need to destroy this place now."

"No." He looked at Kate when she voiced her opinion. Before he could tell her she didn't get a vote, she moved toward him and the building. "What if we can go there? I mean, what if this is the only way we can end this once and for all? Go there and destroy whatever is making these things and end this?"

"You really think that it'll be that easy?" Rick looked at him when Kate didn't have an answer for his question. "I agree that we might not want to destroy it yet, but going there? I'm not sure that's a good idea either. Hector said that in order to go there and remain in one piece that you had to be on death's bed. I don't know about you guys, but I kind of like living. Even with all this other crap going on, this is better than being dead."

After talking to Remy it was decided in the end that they'd not destroy the building, but they'd put people there to stop anyone else from entering. Hector was coming to check it out, along with Remy and Skylar and the rest of the men and women, but Chris didn't like it. It was just too...he didn't think it was scary, but more horrific than that. Who the hell were these people, and why did they want them all dead?

"You do not trust this?" Chris looked at Cobb. There was something very odd about the man, and he wasn't really sure he trusted him either. "I should like to think that there is good in all people, but lately, there seems to be nothing but death and mayhem. Don't you agree? I know that you have no reason to trust me, but I will tell you that I shall never harm those that are in alliance with Kate. She is...she will be very protective of those that she considers her family or friends."

His voice, his words. There was something there, but Chris couldn't put his finger on it. When Remy was stressed or tired, he'd slip back into an old world speech, but this man...Chris thought the man was out of touch.

"I don't know what to think." Which was true. "How long have you been out here? On your own, I mean?"

"You don't have to trust me, young man." Cobb laughed when Chris started to deny it. "I'm not from around here. I am of earth, but...I'm nearly as old as your Hector. I have lived here through many changes...too many I guess, so that I went to ground. Not unlike a vampire, but I hid away. Then the lady of the earth, she begged me to come and see what was going on, and I have been watching things for her. Your young friend there, the one called Vicki, she's like me. Faerie. We are one and the same but for our age."

"Does she know that?" Cobb said that he had not told anyone but him what he was for a long time. His kind, like most, were hunted. And in that, destroyed because they didn't understand them. "And why me? What makes you think I need to know?"

"Because, my dear friend, you are going to be the one that keeps us safe. Your inner beast, he is stronger than you allow him to be." Chris asked him what he meant. "When the time comes, you will see that I'm correct. Your cat, he is not alone in there, is he?"

34

"I'm just a panther, nothing more." Cobb only nodded. "You know, I'm sick of people giving me half answers. What the fuck do you mean?"

"That when you and she come together, she will give you all you need to come to your own. I cannot tell you more than that. But when she comes to you, and she will, you will know a strength that none before you nor after will ever know again. You will be...what does Rick call it? Ah yes. You will be awesomesauce." Cobb laughed and nodded at him as Chris just stood there. He wanted to ask who *she* was, but was afraid that he knew that too.

When Cobb left him, Chris looked over at Kate. She was talking to Rick and Remy, and he wondered not for the first time what she was doing here. What was her deal? As they moved toward one of the vehicles that Hector had brought with him when he'd come here, he ended up sitting in the front and her in the back. Chris decided that he was going to avoid her now. At all costs. There wasn't any way that she was his mate, but he didn't want to come to her any more than he was sure she wanted to come to him. Whatever the hell that meant.

Chapter 3

Master moved around the little lab and tried again to figure out what he was seeing. He'd been in this other realm for nearly a month now, and he knew that whatever he was looking at was some sort of key. The human behind him called to him again, and Master picked up Dolin's head and went to him. Dolin was the only man he trusted. Then Ward, but Dolin first and foremost.

"Sir?"

The man kept looking at Dolin. Master wondered if he knew the man was dead, and that without a body, he wasn't going to talk to him. Of course, Dolin spoke to him. It was how he'd known to turn on the switch that brought the others to him; this man being one of them. Master wanted to think it was his idea, but really, the big green switch had nearly screamed at him to turn it to the other direction. Master realized the man was still staring at Dolin.

He'd had to put Dolin in a sort of netting. About a week ago, while he'd been carrying around his only friend by his hair, Master had dropped him. The hair, like a lot of the other things on Dolin's head, had simply fallen off, leaving a large bald space where it had been. Dolin's nose, along with one of his ears, had come up missing a few days ago. Now Master carried him in a net so that not only were his parts all there, but he was easier to transport when he needed to go elsewhere. Things were needed, and Dolin helped him with the answers.

"What is it? Do you not see I have things to do?" Master really had nothing to do. He was actually in too much pain to do more than just hobble around all the time. But when he sat for too long, he nearly sobbed until he worked some of the pain out of his joints and muscles. His body would stiffen up and the muscles would cramp up when he tried to stand again. The pain was overwhelming at times. "What did you want?"

"I've figured out the formula. I mean, I think I have. I'm not really sure."

Master wanted to hug him, but remained where he was in the event that the nasty word followed. They, the three men that he had here now, were forever saying that they'd done this or that, but it was always followed by the word "but." There was always a *but*. Master giggled at his thought, and that had the man staring at him now. Master asked him what he had to do now.

"I was just going to try it out on him when I thought you should know. The preliminary tests show that it's just the right mixture of—" Master told him to finish and give him the results. "You said I could leave when I figured it out. You promised me. Before I try this out and it works, I want to know that you will uphold your end of the bargain. You will, right? Let me go like you said."

"So I did. But we've no way of knowing if this one works any better than the last one, do we? You've all told me before that you had it, and it was nothing more than a thing to put me to sleep. He paid the price for that, didn't he?" They both looked at the man that had disappointed Master earlier in the week. He supposed that his body should have been stacked with the rest, but Master thought it was a good reminder to do what he wanted. No one messed with him, and he liked it that way. "Test it. I've not got all day while you wait on something else."

He limped to the man that they'd found wandering the streets. He wasn't right in the head. Master had wanted to kill him right away when he'd come upon him, but Dolin had suggested that they'd needed a test subject, and what better person than him? Dolin, since his death, was a much smarter man than when he'd been living, as far as Master was concerned.

The man in the cage screamed when they came toward him, cowering in the corner as far away as he was able. Master had noticed that he'd begun to not eat yesterday, and now it seemed he was defecating in his food bowls. Well, he'd have to eat that now...Master was not going to clean up after him. As the man was pulled to the bars and injected, Master watched him to see what, if anything, happened. He'd been sorely disappointed so much of late. And he couldn't wait much longer on his medicine. He was nearly out of it, again.

He knew now that the other creature was dead. When he'd not shown up for several days, Master had gone to the other realm to see what had happened and had found his body, broken and beaten on the ground. Master had been so angered by it that he'd gone to the cave that he'd shared with the other man and started to destroy everything he could touch. Then he found the container, and had nearly tossed it away when he heard it rattle. Master had found the stash that Randall had hidden from him.

There had been sixty vials when he opened it. A few had been broken, but not many. He'd been so mad at Randall that he'd gone back to the man's body and pissed on him. Randall had told him over and over that they were down to a dozen vials, and that he'd taken to only giving Master the drug when he was near death. Well, as near death as he could fake. But now he knew that Randall had lied to him.

The first thing he'd done when he'd found them was shot himself full of the drug with ten of the needles. It might have been a little much, Master thought with a grin. He'd been out for several days, but when he woke, he wasn't feeling any better. After that, he carefully gave himself two of the needles per day, and only when he was feeling poorly did he double that. But still, even after rationing things out, he was nearly out of the drug. Master had a feeling that someone was there, taking his drug without his permission, but as yet, he'd not been able to find him. When the amount of drugs was getting dangerously low, Dolin had helped him with the switch. The switch that had brought him—

"It's working." Master pulled himself from his thoughts when the man next to him sounded so excited. He looked in the direction that he was and saw that the man in the cage had changed somewhat. "Look, it's working on him."

It seemed to be. But the real test, and one that he so enjoyed, was to see how the man reacted to pain. Reaching out to the man, Master snapped his arm off and watched in glee as he lay there in his own blood and shit and smiled at him. It was perfect.

"I need you to make me as much as you can." The man—his lab coat said Ward, but Master knew he'd only borrowed it—was shaking his head. "You cannot tell me that you've no idea how to remake this. I have told you over and over to write it down. Even Dolin has said as much to you. Make me as much as you can with what you have here and I shall get you.... Why are you still shaking your head at me?"

The man looked over at Dolin and shivered as his head continued to shake. "You said I could leave once I figured out the compound. You promised. I have a family there. I need to see to them."

"Ah yes, so I did. But you'll be happy to know that I've taken care of them. They're dead and no longer in need of you. So you can make my drug without thinking about them any longer. I need you more than they did anyway. You must know that." The man backed from him and Master wanted to kill him. But he knew, as he'd learned from Dolin, that killing the man that helped you was not a good idea. "What is it now? You need more money? I assure you that you've no need of anything else. I have jewels that you can have. And as for your family, you are better off without them. They were draining you dry anyway. Always making demands on you and your time."

"You killed them?" Master nodded, not really seeing the problem. He did glance at Dolin to see if he was watching this, and turned his head so that he could see it as well. The things that he had to put up with was making him angry. "You walk around here talking to a dead man's head, and you just expect me to be all right with you killing my family? What is wrong with you? You made a promise to me and now you've broken it by...by killing them. Seriously, what the fuck is wrong with you?"

"Nothing." Master let a little of his beast go. It was painful and draining on him, but the man in front of him had no way of knowing just how weak he was. And if he did, he'd soon find out that no one messed with Master. "Do as I say or I shall kill you."

"No."

Master killed him. There was no hope for it, and he was sure that the dead man would know that as soon as he thought things through. As he lay there bleeding, Master waited for him to come to his senses. But the longer he lay there, his body simply not moving, Master wondered when anyone was going to do as he told them without him having to resort to violence. Nothing was going as he had planned it, and it was all Rembrandt's fault. He'd told him time and time again to let him kill him, and still he lived.

When there was nothing more forthcoming from the man on the floor, he turned to the last man with him, one of the few that had come through the portal when Dolin had told him to turn on the green switch. He didn't trust this man any more than he did the others, but he was all that he had for now. The man only stared at the man on the floor, saying nothing at all.

"You'll make it for me now. As you can see, I've no need for men who do not do as they're told. You'll get started on what I want without hesitation." The man looked at him and smiled. "You think I jest with you? I assure you that I am not."

"No, I believe you. You look like a...man, I guess, who gets what he wants or else. I do understand that. But you should know that whatever he invented, I'm pretty sure that it's dead with him. He only wrote down the formula after it was injected in the test subject so that he'd not do it again. So we have a bunch of not working recipes, and not one that he got to work."

Master let his beast take him. His anger was so profound that he knew for several minutes that he'd lost control. This was all Rembrandt's fault; everything that had happened fell on the steps of his worst enemy. Rembrandt had fucked him over and over, again and again.

When he awoke—that's how he'd begun to think of his rages when they happened—he was in the shelter where he'd found Dolin hiding. He was also alone. Standing up, always painful nowadays, had him staggering out of the shelter and into the dark inky night. Stars, it seemed, had forsaken him as well as he looked up into the sky to see where he might have been. As he made his way to the labs, he wondered what sort of destruction he'd find there, and wasn't surprised to find the doors torn off their hinges and several of the front windows gone as well.

Bricks and glass were strewn everywhere. He knew on some level that he'd done this, but his mind was fuzzy on the details as to why or how he had. As he made his way to the lower levels he took note of the things that Rembrandt had caused him to do, and knew that for each thing, there was going to be payment made to him. Master had had enough of the man. He'd been his ruination since the moment he'd been turned that day.

"I cannot believe that it has come to this. Me having to work in these kinds of conditions. Broken items, glass on the floor. Why will no one just do as I say?" He stepped over a wall, not a door but an entire wall, to enter what was left of his lab. Dolin, he thought, had been down here, so he looked for him before anything else. "Dolin? Where are you? Dolin?"

"You killed him." Master turned so quickly that he fell. His body, most of which had been damaged too much to heal, was not able to withstand quick movements any more. But as he lay there in the glass and broken test tubes, he looked at the man standing above him. "Hello, Augustus. I see you've been up to your usual tricks. Why is it you let your temper get the better of you?"

"Rembrandt, how did you get here?" He looked around for a weapon and Rembrandt laughed at him. "I should like to kill you now. Come here. I shall end this now."

"I'm not with you, but a figment of your mind. It's about gone, you know...your mind. Not that you had a great deal of it before. But now, you've lost it. Why else would you be thinking of me at this moment?" Master started to tell him he was just fine when he morphed; Rembrandt just changed into that woman, the one that had tried to kill Master several times. "See? You can't even hold onto your enemies long enough to try and kill them. You're insane. And you stink as well. Did you know that?"

"I'm no such thing. And I do not smell. Even if I did, you said you were not here, so how do you know? Lies. All lies." He looked around again for something to smash her face in when she laughed at him. "You will come here now and help me to my feet. I will kill you, there is no hope for it, but I will not allow you to laugh at me."

The next person to be standing before him was Ward. He was just as pompous looking as he'd been before Randall had ripped his head off. Master tried again to have him help him from the floor. He was nicer to him...Master was really aching to stand, and thought Ward was the only one who would do it.

"I'm not able to help you get up for the same reasons that the other two could not. I'm not here. But I have

44

decided to help you. The formula that you want, you can do this." Master asked him how. "There are about ten vials left, correct? You saved ten of them for yourself?"

"I had to use two today, but there are six." Ward told him his adding was off, but Master told him to go on with his idea. Of course there were eight left, but if Ward thought to take them, then he'd at least have the two. "Tell me how to make this drug that you're talking about. Surely you can see that I have no one left here to make it for me."

"He didn't write it down, you said, but he did write down the ones that didn't work, right? You can use those to get to the one that does. Just don't do those again. You need to get started on those." Master hated to say it, but he told Ward that it would matter little, since he could not read it anyway. "Ah. Then get one of the others to come here and do it. The portal is open still, right?"

It was. Where were...he had no idea what was going on that had brought the first group of men here, but when they appeared in the little room that had been closed off to him when he'd been here, he'd been excited to see them. He knew it had to do with the switch he'd turned, but nothing more. He asked Ward why there had been no more people coming here to help him.

"Rembrandt did it." Master nodded. Of course he did. He'd been messing with his plans for years now. "Go there and see what happened. You can do it. Just don't let them see you. And while you're there, find someone that can read and write and get them to come back here with you. You are Master, are you not?"

"I am; yes. I am. Excellent plan." He started to stand and realized that he needed to clean himself up. Even if no one saw him, Master liked to look good. And he would have to try and stay as this self. Shifting to his beast, even as much as he loved him, was going to harm him in ways that he would not recover from. He understood this now. Without his medicine, he would have to be careful where he tread from now on.

There had to be clothing here. Not anything that he would normally wear, but there was no cleaning staff here to clean up after him so he had to wear what he could find. Mostly it had been Dolin's things, but right now he knew that he needed something that made him look powerful. Going to the shelter again, he found himself in Ward's rooms.

There were things there that he'd never wear. A large sweater that had some sort of animal on it. There were pants too, soft ones that were so bright with color that Master decided that he'd rather not be seen glowing with them on. Finally, he settled on a nice soft shirt and some pants that were a little snug, but fit him well enough. He was ready to go when he realized that he had left Dolin behind. He needed his friend now, if for no other reason than to keep him from being too lonely.

It took him an hour to find Dolin in the mess that had been made. And Master was saddened to see that his friends head had been split open at some point and now he was no longer able to travel with him. Another thing to blame on Rembrandt and that woman. The list was getting very long, and as soon as he had his drugs and them where he wanted them, he was going to list each item before he extracted payment for it. They would understand that this had to be done.

"Those people are going to pay for this and I will enjoy it." Master didn't have a clear plan on how to make them pay, but they would. As he made his way to the little place where he could travel between worlds, he thought of something he'd seen in the other world. A recording device. He had to find one of those so that he could put his list to words, his own words to keep things straight. "I will need to have Ward or one of the men I bring back tell me how to make it work. Such things have been a mystery to me for too long."

He moved through the portal and landed near the cave that he'd spent so much time in. Master was glad for it really; the travel had exhausted him too much to walk much more, and he knew that he'd have to go to wherever the green switch had worked. Going into the cave, he lay on the ground and closed his eyes. Later he would find out about the portal, get him some men, and kill Rembrandt and that woman. Things would work out, he just knew it.

~~~

Chris was sitting in the entertainment room when Kate walked in. It had been three days since she'd been brought here, and she didn't seem to be any happier about it now than she had then. He was pretty sure he knew how she felt, but he did need to speak with her. When she saw him, he stopped her when she turned to leave him.

"Please, don't go. I'd like a word with you, if you don't mind." She asked him what he could possibly want. "I'm not really sure what I want, but I would like to ask you a few questions. What are you, for starters?"

"I don't see what that has to do with anything going on around here." He guessed that she was right, but it didn't make him want to know any less. "What are you?"

"Panther, as I'm sure you know. And a little more. The more part I don't know how to explain, as most of this shit is just coming to us as we fumble around. But you seem to not only know what you are, but have a handle on it too. I just...can't you just answer the question for once?" He watched her and knew that she was struggling with whether or not she wanted to stay or leave. "Please? Sit down and talk to me."

"I'm a shifter. Elite shifter. Nate, that other guy that no one sees, he is one too. But I think I have a little more than him. I'm older too. Even older than you are." He nodded. Chris had no idea, but he had thought she was older the other day when she'd been talking to Ana in the kitchen. "Does that satisfy your curiosity?"

"No. Not really. I know what an elite shifter is, but what is the more?" He was glad when she sat down. It meant that she wasn't going to bolt again. "And just how old are you?"

"It's considered rude to ask a woman her age, isn't it?" He grinned at her, and she, unlike most women he knew, didn't seem to be charmed by it. In fact, he thought it pissed her off. "I'm over four hundred and twenty years old. I've been through a few decades and have had time to practice things that come to me with age. The more is what my husband gave me before...he gave me all that he was when he took me as his mate."

"Does he know where you are?" Kate told him that her mate was dead. "I'm sorry. So is mine. She died a few years ago when I drove the two of us over a cliff. She and my unborn son were killed."

"I didn't really care for my mate. He was...he wasn't a nice person. Not most of the time, anyway. Then one day, right before we were to go on a long trip together, to see his family as a matter of fact, he was taken away in chains and hung in the town square. It was said that they did all witches that way, but he wasn't one. Not wholly anyway." He wondered what the not wholly meant, but before he could ask her, she spoke again. "What was your mate?"

"Human. Or mostly human...I don't think she was aware that she had a little magic in her. I meant to tell her, but we never got...conversations were not high on our list when fighting was so much easier. We began our marriage well enough, I guess. She was older than me, and smarter. Or so she kept telling me." He waited for Kate to tell him that everyone was smarter than him, but she only stared at him. "Anyway, her father didn't care all that much for me from the very start. I mean, he made no bones about it. He was under the impression that she could have done a great deal better than me. I guess she could have, but we were happy, for a time I guess. Then when we found out that she was going to have a baby, things sort of changed."

He got up to go to the little fridge that seemed to be in every room he was in. Chris drank about twenty to fifty bottles of ice cold water every day. More if they were working. After he drained the bottle and tossed the container in the trash, he offered Kate one. When she took it, he sat down again, but this time on the same sofa she was on.

"They had money." He turned to Kate and nodded when she said that. "She married you to get back at her dad...you know that, don't you?"

"I kinda figured that out after the fact. But she was going to have my baby, and I figured I could put up with a great deal for a child. We were mates." Kate shook her head, and he sat there while she made her way to him, scooting along the sofa as she did. "Our kind can't have children by anyone but our mates."

"Maybe so, but did it ever occur to you that it wasn't your child? She wasn't what you are, so there was no reason for her to not have a child by another man, was there?" He didn't answer her. He had thought about that a great deal. But as she touched her fingers to his chest, right where his heart was, he held his breath while she pressed her fingers into him. "Your heart is pure. Untouched by love, yet filled with sorrow and anger. You're angry more than you are hurt, aren't you, Chris?"

"I never said I loved her. Only that she was my mate. I don't think either of us uttered those words the entire time we were together, as a matter of fact." Kate moved back to her side of the sofa and Chris felt the loss profoundly. He wanted her to be close to him again...he wanted— "How did you know that? I mean, what did you feel when you touched me?"

"That there is no love in your heart. If you let me search through your mind, I can also tell you about the accident you said that the two of you were in. I doubt very much you were the cause of it." He asked her how she would know that. "Because you don't think you were either. You might have at first, but you don't any longer, do you?"

He didn't say anything. Chris had thought about a lot of things lately. Like Pella's father, and some of the things he'd said to him when they were still at the graveside. He'd demanded that Chris admit to killing his little girl and to not take the insurance money. There had been a great deal of it too. Chris hadn't touched it, but turned it over to the local hospital to have a children's burn unit built in Pella's name. That too had sent Pella's father over the edge. Enough so that he'd dragged him to court several times before all of this happened.

"I don't guess it matters anymore." Kate said it did to him. "If I let you do this, what do you get out of it?"

"I don't want anything from you." She stood up. "I don't even want to be here, but until Remy is satisfied that I'm not part of the problem, I'm stuck here."

When she left him, Chris leaned back on the sofa again. He had a feeling that he was going to regret not having her tell him what he might already know. That there had been a second car on the hillside, and that he'd been avoiding it rather than driving like a fool as he'd been told he had been. Yes, he'd been driving fast, but not stupid. The roads were dry, not wet as he'd been told, and there had been someone else on that windy road other than him and Pella.

They'd been arguing. Loudly and viciously. She'd told him — not for the first time — that her daddy would help her leave him if he didn't do whatever it was she wanted at that moment. Chris told her that she should leave him, but she wasn't taking his child with her. Her laughter and her next words had caused him to look away from the road, just for a moment, and when he looked back he saw the other car.

"There wasn't another car. You killed her. You murdered her and my grandchild." Chris had heard those words spoken to him almost the moment he opened his eyes and asked about Pella and the other driver. Martin Webster had been standing over his bed screaming at him that he'd killed his only child. And a grandson that would have been so much better than his supposed father.

"The other driver, I saw him." Martin had hit him then, hard enough to knock him off the gurney he'd been on and into a nurse. "I want to see my wife. Now...I need to see her."

"You killed her. You killed my little girl."

The memory of that day, like so many after, had haunted him. Daily almost. But as he sat there, his heart in his hand, he thought of Kate, and realized in that moment that the memory of what he'd done had not haunted him since he'd met her. And he wondered on that for the rest of the night.

Chapter 4

Hector looked at the dead creature and wondered who had sent it. Kate had explained to him that she'd seen several of them recently. And Hector had had to explain that they were from his world, and that he'd had no idea that they'd been brought here.

"They're birds of prey, Merriam's teratorn. Or that's what we called them long ago. We have not used them in our world for killing for a great many years. I would have thought, if asked, that they were all dead. Perhaps Dolin or Ward have sent them in an effort to kill us." He had said to Remy just this morning he needed to go back to the other world to check on things. Now he had to make it a priority. "I shall find out from them what I can."

"You do know that this is some fucked up information." Hector, now that he had been here for a while, was beginning to understand some of the things that they said to him, and knew that this was not a question that Skylar expected an answer for. "How the hell do we win this thing if more and more shit keeps popping up all the time?"

"I'm sorry."

He was too. Everyday Hector regretted everything that had happened to these people. Mostly the ones in the encampment where he was now staying with his son, but all the deaths in both their worlds, too. He'd found out recently that he'd not created the monsters that were plentiful here, but he did still feel bad for the deaths that they'd caused. It seemed that what they'd done had been a mistake from the very beginning.

"I shall see if I can find out how many they have sent. Miss Kate has said she's killed three of them; perhaps that is all of them."

"I doubt it." So did he, but he only nodded at Remy when he spoke. "When do you leave to see the other world? And I want to tell you again how much I hate you going there. It's not safe for you. You have no idea what might be waiting for you on the other side. Nor if the portal that you use is even safe any longer."

"I am very careful. And they do not see me until I can be assured that it is safe for me to show myself. As for the portal, if I cannot use it, it will simply not let me enter on this end. It's a failsafe that I have put in when I was there last. Perhaps I will find that Ward and Dolin are both dead, and that Benton has died as well." That, too, wasn't something he was counting on. Evil people seldom did what was right. "I will leave now if you do not mind. I have a list of things that I need to procure as well. Some plants that I think will help with things here, and if I can, I'd like to bring back a few of the drugs there as well. Things that perhaps Weston can break down and see what they are made of. Some of which I think will cure a great many things that have killed before this. I am working with Weston, a fine doctor by the way, and he is most pleased for me to bring things back for him to study."

He'd been having long conversations with the doctor lately. Weston was a brilliant doctor and surgeon, and since they'd brought him help, he had more time to experiment with some of the items they'd been able to find for him. A few of them that the malefactors had been turned with had been analyzed several times, and they were working on a cure for them.

The agate had been the biggest find for them all. Not that the people found much use for it here, but in his realm, it had been as valuable as gold was here. Dolin and Ward had used them to convert some of the malefactors into stronger and meaner killing machines. Now...well, he wasn't sure what they were doing, other than resurrecting things that had long since died out. And that was making him think they were getting desperate.

After telling Ruben he would return soon and that he'd look for some of the items on his own list, Hector made his way to the portal. There hadn't been one before on this property, but he had set one up the last time he'd been to the other world. Remy thought it a good idea; that way no one could come back with him that they didn't want to. Anything that came through it without permission would die. Anyone with ill will or murder on their mind would also die. It was a safety net that Remy had insisted on and Hector loved. Remy, for all his old world ways, was a very brilliant man, Hector thought.

The first thing he saw when he exited the portal was destruction. Not the kind of destruction that one would find in a developing neighborhood, but things were destroyed in a way that made him think there had been a great deal of anger in it. Just as he was bending to see what was shining back at him on the ground in the otherwise desolate area, he saw Benton moving in his direction.

Hector was shocked at what he looked like. Not only did the man look as if he'd been chewed up and spit out, a term that Vicki had taught him, but he'd been chewed in a way that made him look as if he was close to his own death. Laying low while keeping an eye on the creature, he listened to what he was saying. The man seemed to be having a conversation with Ward. But as far as Hector could see, there was no one with him.

"I know that's what you said, but I've no way of making that work. You know that, as I have repeated myself several times on the matter by now." The long pause made Hector think that Benton was listening to the phantom Ward talk. "Yes, yes. I get it. If we kill them then we can have all the stones we want and build an army of my men. But I have to be able to make the drugs first. I've only just a few left, and that's not enough if that bitch tries to burn me again with her evil magic."

Benton moved around the area, circling around and around like he was looking for something. Hector did as well. Whatever the man wanted, he wanted it too. Then he remembered the shining object and looked around until he found it.

It was a vial of something clear. The needle was bent in an odd way, but the cylinder was full of the liquid. Putting it in the pouch that he'd brought with him, Hector watched and listened to Benton. It was then that he realized that he was looking for what Hector had found.

"I know that you say you didn't take it, Ward, but where is it if you don't have it? That medicine is all that I have to keep me from hurting. I hurt all the time now, thanks to Rembrandt. I need it. Randall thought to keep if all from me, but you know how smart I am, and that was his downfall." Benton limped by him, dragging his long arm behind him as he did. "I need to find a way to make more of it, and then I will be master of all there is to see. That and only that will keep me from being killed when I go back there. And then I'm going to kill Rembrandt. Did I tell you I was there recently? They have a nice place, and here I live with nothing. Not even a clean bed. I, master of all, have been reduced to living in a cave where there is nary a stone to keep me warm."

Hector wondered where the cave was, but concentrated on what Benton was saying. It seemed like gibberish, but he pulled out his note pad and began writing as quickly as he could. His handwriting was very neat most of the time, but right now he didn't care so long as he got it all. Hector knew that this was going to be helpful to them all once they figured out what he was talking about.

Benton kept going on about finding his meds. Hector had no idea what the drug would have done to him, or for him, for that matter, but there was no way that he was going to help him by giving it to him. Whatever it was, he was sure it was bad for them. There had to be a way to make something to do the opposite of what this thing did, and he was going to see if Weston could produce it for them.

After another twenty minutes or so, Benton moved on, not finding the vial that Hector now had. Hector got up from his hiding place and made his way around the neighborhood. It took him ten more minutes of wandering around to realize that he was in Dolin's neighborhood, and that the rubble in front of him had at one time been the man's home. Going over the area, he found what he thought was the shelter that the two of them, Dolin and Ward, had been hiding in when he'd come here to scare them. It was much like the one that Jamey had lived in when she'd been hiding out in the other realm.

That was where he found the body of Ward. Or what was left of him. His head had been torn from his body, but there was no sign of it in the shelter. The man had been tossed aside as if he were no more than a rag that had been soiled. Hector was almost afraid to go to Ward's home, or what was left of it, fearful of what he might find there as well.

He'd not cared for either man toward the end. Both of them had killed his lovely wife, and had tried to do the same to his little boy. From the start they'd led him to believe that he'd been responsible for the creatures that the other realm had been fighting. He'd begun to keep his notes on projects that he worked on in secret, even going as far as to have two sets...one for the office, and the other that he'd had hidden at his home. And it turned out that not only were they the ones that had done it, but the two of them were related in some way.

Ward's home was in worse shape than Dolin's. The walls that had been made entirely of glass were shattered into such small pieces that it looked like sand. His furniture, always the best for Ward, was nothing more than puffs of cotton hanging from dead or dying trees and on the grass. It sort of reminded him of flowers in the spring. Shaking his head at the senselessness of it all, he moved to where he knew a beautiful garden had once been planted, hoping for a few plants to save.

He found some plants that he'd been looking for. He also managed to find a few boxes and a spade that he could dig them up with. There were flowers there too, most of which he was sure would grow in the other world, and he wondered briefly what sort of colors they'd get in the other soil. He took these boxes to the portal to await his return to the other realm.

Most of the gardens around the homes, like them, had been knocked over. He wondered, just a little, what sort of thing had done this, and didn't want to dwell too much on it being Benton. The man had been insane before this, and he wondered if it had gotten worse. Well, he supposed he knew it had gotten worse, but how badly was anyone's guess.

There were no bodies at most of the other houses, thankfully. There were no bodies much anywhere, now that he made his way to the labs. Hector was amazed at the contrasts of things here. A flower garden in full bloom, their buds nearly a foot off the ground, was surrounded by so much destruction that it was amazing that something as delicate as them had survived at all. A playground, devoid of children, was in pristine condition, yet all around it trees were toppled, their roots like large spiders climbing from the dirt. A house stood as if it had only just been built between two that looked like someone large had simply stepped on them, crushing them to the dirt. Destruction on a mass scale was everywhere.

The lab was in worse shape than the homes surrounding it. The windows had been broken out, pieces of them sparkling brightly in the afternoon sun like diamonds. Papers were flying about, most of which made no sense whatsoever to him, and after gathering a few of them, he let them go. Vials had been thrown about; lab coats, most of which were stained with a dark rust that he knew as blood, were flapping in the wind like a kite on a warm summer day. Hector smiled at the thought, how so many things reminded him of things he and his son now did. But then he entered the lab proper.

The smell of death permeated the air. It was thick with it, so thick that he wanted to turn and leave. It was strong enough to cause him to gag, and he had second thoughts as to whether or not there would be anything there that he might need. But he knew that some of what he had said he'd find, things that he wanted to bring out, were below where he stood, so he covered his mouth and nose with his shirt and moved deeper into the building.

The bodies had been stacked up in tall piles around the rooms. Most of them had been dead for a long time if their decomposition was any indication. He would not have been able to tell anyone who the people were but for their names on their lab coats. Even those were stained so badly that it would be nearly impossible to tell what they might have said at one time. But as he moved on, going to the labs, he wondered what sort of terrible mess he'd find there.

Broken glass and doors torn from hinges met him, and even the tables had been bent double. Their use, if one were to enter this room for the first time, would be unknown. Cabinets that had at one time been neatly filled, labels stuck to the front so he could easily find what he wanted, were now nothing more than broken glass and steel, the items that they'd once held no longer safe within their confines. Even the equipment was torn up, broken beyond repair. Walls were embedded with surgical tools, glass, and even...he thought it was bone. Hector did not want to think about the force it had taken to do that.

He found Ward's head, decomposed and rotted, sitting upon a table as if he were ruling the room. And this was where he found the body of Dolin, his head also missing. The two men had not been killed easily, it seemed, but perhaps quickly. Again, he wondered at the strength that it would take to tear a man's head from his body like that.

The noise behind him had him moving quickly to a safe place before he was seen. Then when he shadowed himself, making sure that whoever was there could no longer see him, he watched as three men, all of them loyal only to Ward and Dolin, entered the lab. They looked like they had been doing well; their clothing was clean and they didn't look any worse for wear with all that had been going on. He wondered where they were hiding out.

"I tell you, I saw Hector. Plain as day. And he looked fit too, nothing like he did when he was here." The other man, Tony he thought his name was, asked him where he was then. "I don't fucking know. But he's here, and if he's here then things might be turning for us. I can't do this anymore, Buddy. There is no one here to do chores and shit. I've taken to washing my own clothing at the pond down the way. Those women that are there? They told me to do it myself. No respect no more, I'm telling you."

Hector liked that they noticed that he'd been working out. He and Ruben had taken to using the gym. Not so much his son, but he kept him company as he worked. But there was trouble afoot and he had to pay attention.

"Did you see that thing walking around the neighborhood this morning? The one that they'd been working with? Benton, I think his name was. Damn, but there was some messed up crap going on there." Buddy agreed with Tony and they started looking around the lab. "I haven't had a decent meal in about a month that I haven't had to cook for myself. I was eating flowers I found growing in my yard, I'm so hungry, until I found that stash up the way. And that other woman, the one that takes around them meals? She said that we can only have one a day of the shit that she cooks. There isn't much to go around she told me, when I know better. I think she's full of it, and I'm going to go there and steal it all tonight."

Hector thought that he would have a better look around for others like this woman to bring back to the other world. These men would kill their own mother if they could profit from it. He was sorry that food was not plentiful here. But really, he didn't understand that either. There was magic about, and they should have been able to get what they needed to prepare their own meals.

Both of the men had worked in this lab when it had been a fully functioning place. One of them had been his assistant for a time. He knew that Buddy could come up with whatever it was that Benton was talking about if he only tried, and that frightened him just a little. If either of these men wanted, they could put the other realm into more trouble with just a little effort. And that just would not do.

"What's this?" Hector moved closer to see what they were looking at, and he nearly fell back when he saw it. There was another vial there, and this one was full. "Hey, you think this is the shit he's been looking for? You heard him. Something about a drug? I bet it is. I'm betting he'll pay plenty to have it back too, don't you think?"

"Yeah. That's what he was saying. What do you know about this? You think it's something that we can turn a profit on maybe?" Tony turned as Buddy did when something fell over, to see that Benton had joined them.

"We were just leaving." Hector wanted to tell them to run, get out, but Tony was backing up deeper into the building as he continued talking to Benton. "We found this and was going to leave it for you. But we was going out. Okay?"

"I don't think so. You will stay here, do as you're told. But where have you been? Hiding? That's not terribly nice of you, now is it? Do you know if there are others, ones that can serve me while we work?" Neither man moved, nor did Hector as he watched them. Something had been decidedly scary about Benton, even before this whole thing. Now he was fucking scary, as Remy would say. "Come, come. We have work to do. I have something I need for you to do for me."

Hector left the lab when it was apparent that neither man was going to live through this. Benton had lost control of himself twice when they told him that they wanted to leave, and he'd killed Tony and the other man with a swipe of his large clawed hand. Life for Buddy, Hector thought, was not going to be good, and he might wish that he'd been killed instead of his friends before long.

Gathering what he could of the plants and herbs on his land, Hector had his bag full, as well as the several boxes he'd found along the way in his search. He'd even gone back to his home, the one he'd shared with his family, and was surprised to find it just as he'd left it. The food had been taken, of course, even his blankets, but his home looked well. Going through the house he found most of what he wanted, and all from the list that Ruben had asked him for. Pictures of his mother were also put in the several boxes that he was going to take back with him.

Things, flowers, and herbs were just lying about now, most of it neglected to the point where it was dead or dying. But he thought that if he could make even half of the things grow, he'd be able to help the others of the new realm he was living in. He was glad that Remy had made it so that he could bring things with him this time. It would have been hard to do this otherwise.

~~~

Kate watched the children run and play with the little puppies. Even the parents had come out to enjoy the sight, pulling out lawn chairs to sit on and even a few blankets. It would be cold soon, and she would bet that these were the last few days of warm weather they would have for a while.

Chris came and stood beside her, and she turned to leave. "Please don't." She paused and asked him why. "I don't know. I just wanted to talk to you. You and I, we seem to be...I guess last man out. And I wanted to talk to you about what you said yesterday. That is, if you don't mind. I'm sort of lost here, and I think you can help me."

"I said a great many things yesterday, Chris. Not as many as most, but I did speak." He laughed and told her it was about the accident. "I see. And are you ready to think on what really happened, or are you still mired in grief? I can't help you if you don't believe me. But I think you know that."

"I don't know that there was much in the way of grief for my wife, if you want to know the truth. For my child, if it was mine, but not for her. I think for a long time before the accident, I figured we were not suited. But how did you know?" She didn't say anything, because she was pretty sure that he knew the answer to that as well. "I think her father killed her and blamed me because it didn't end the way he'd hoped. It was me he wanted dead, not her, and he hired those men—the ones that he said weren't there—to do it for him."

"You know the answer to that as well as I do, don't you? Do you remember the accident?" He said that he had always remembered it. "Then you wish for me to look? To see what you couldn't before? I promise you, there will be no pain for you. I'll just look at what you saw and felt that day."

"I think so...I do. I want to know. The grief, as you said, is killing me. Not for the death, but that I might have caused it." She nodded and asked him when. "I don't know. Do you have to have some sort of dark room? Maybe I have to lie down?"

"No, you're fine this way." The thought of him lying down made her body warm. It had been a very long time since she'd had any desire for a male. More so since her body had seemed to wake for a touch. Reaching out her hand, just to touch his head, she moaned slightly when he put his hand over hers. "Don't. You can't touch me like this. I can't think."

"Yes you can. Like me, you just don't want to think." He pulled her closer. It did work better, her ability to see into his mind, if they were close, but they didn't need to be body to body as they were now. "I can smell you. You're warming to me. Your body is responding to mine the way that mine is to you."

Closing her eyes against the onslaught of feelings he was pulling from her, Kate tried to concentrate on what she could find. As soon as she found the deep memories, her body stiffened when his did.

"You were arguing." He said that they always were. "You believed then that the child was not yours. You asked her about it that day. It was why you were arguing. She finally told you the truth."

"She said that it wasn't. I'd forgotten about that until now. She told me that I'd been taken, that not only wasn't the kid mine, but she wasn't planning to keep it either." Kate wrapped her arm around his shoulders when he lifted her to his body, his cock to her pussy, her breasts to his chest. "Tell me what you see. I need to...I need to know."

"There was a car. It was fast, coming at you from the opposite direction." Chris said that he saw it every time he closed his eyes, but he'd been told there was no one else. "Two men were in the front, one in the back. See them? They were on the wrong side of the road, in your lane, as you came around the bend. They knew you were there, you thought. Not only that, but you had a feeling that they were there to kill you all."

"I don't think they stopped or slowed when they saw us. I think...I think that Pella knew; she smiled when I told her to brace herself." Kate told him that they hadn't slowed down. Then to show him, she paused his memories on the faces of the men in the front. "They knew us. I know them. They worked for her father, Pella's father. And they were there to kill us."

"They ran you off the road. But you swerved in the other direction, into the hillside, instead of the other side where the embankment was, taking the impact on your side and not your wife's." Chris said that it had put them in a tailspin, tossing them all over the road until they hit the guardrail. "Pella was hit by their car when it came back around; they'd been put in a free for all as well. When your car swung around to them again, they rammed their car into your wife's side and she took the brunt of the accident rather than you. It was not the way that they had planned it. Both men in the front were hurt, but they managed to drive away."

"So they hit us hoping to kill me and not her. But why?" Kate pulled her hand away and he stopped her before she could pull her body away too. "Don't leave me. I want...I don't know what I want, but I don't want to be alone. Talk to me. I know you know more than this. What happened to those men? Someone would have been pissed that things didn't go as planned. Where did they go?"

"They're all dead. All three of them were killed by your father-in-law as soon as he found out from them that you'd lived but his daughter had not. Had the child lived, he would have been satisfied...bringing up the child in his image would have been fine with him. But his daughter and grandchild both were killed that day." He nodded. "The child...you know now that it wasn't yours. That she was trying to have you raise another man's child. At least until her father came around or killed you. Which she was hoping for from the start."

"I would have raised him as my own. Gladly. Not for her, but because...because whoever the man was, he wasn't going to be in his life and I was." Kate nodded, her body still wrapped up in his. "Will you let me kiss you, Kate?"

"I don't think that's a good idea, do you? I mean, we don't even like each other." He leaned closer, his breath warm and sweet against her mouth. "I have to tell you something. You might already know."

"You're my mate." She nodded. "Yeah, I'm a little slow, but I figured it out this morning when I was in the shower and thought about you and connected. I can only do that with my mate, and I was never able to do that with Pella. I thought...well, it matters little what I thought now. But I do want to kiss you."

"Because of the changes in our bodies you can tell that we're one." He asked her what had happened to her. "Sigils are where there were none before...not a great many, but a few of them. I have strength that I didn't before, as well as...oh, Chris. Will you please kiss me?"

"Gladly. But that's not what I meant." He brushed his mouth gently over hers. It was quick, unsatisfying, yet made her know that there was a great deal more. "I meant about your mate. You said that you didn't suit."

"He was my mate, but not all of them are fairy book happy. Mine wasn't. He hated me as much as I did him. Ben was a hateful and mean man who thought the world owed him everything because he was who he thought he was." He told her his wasn't either as he kissed her again. This time he took her lower lip into his mouth and nibbled while he lifted her up by her ass and turned with her in his arms. "Are we going somewhere?"

"To my bed." Nodding, Kate moved her mouth to his throat, tasting his warm skin while he took the stairs two at a time. She wasn't sure where his rooms were, but they seemed too far away all of a sudden. "You're going to make it so we don't get there if you keep that up. Not that I want you to quit, but Christ almighty woman, I need you." Kate couldn't help it, she giggled.

As soon as they were in the room, her clothing just disappeared. Kate supposed that she might have taken them off or he had, but there was no time to dwell on such mundane things right now. When he touched her, ran his fingers down her throat to her breast, Kate felt her nipple pucker tightly until it was the most painful pleasure she'd ever felt.

"I want to see all of you. Touch you as well, but I want to see you." Kate nodded and then moaned, closing her eyes when he leaned to her and took her breast into his mouth. His teeth were sharp, grazing the tip of her nipple until he suckled it into his mouth hard. When he lifted his head and smiled at her, it was all she could do not to beg him to do it again.

"Please, I need you." She was wet. Kate could feel her juices as they moved slowly down her thigh. Squeezing her legs together, she heard him chuckle slightly and opened her eyes to look at him.

"You cannot hide from me." When he dropped to his knees in front of her, she nearly came from just seeing him there. "I'm going to enjoy this. More than I think I ever dreamed I would."

She was too. And when he slid his fingers into her, Kate came. It was the first climax she'd ever had, and she was glad now that this man was the one to bring it to her.

Chapter 5

Chris tasted her, feasted on her like he'd never eaten before, neither meal nor woman. He supposed, in a way, he hadn't. Now with his mate, he knew the real meaning of sex, of tasting a woman, of his woman. As she curled her fingers into his hair, holding him to her, Chris marveled at her scent, her taste, and wondered why he'd not realized what she was to him sooner. But even as he drank from her, he was sure that there had never been another before they'd come together, and no one would ever come after her.

"Chris. Please, I can't stand up any more. I need to sit down, lie down. Please?" He knew that her legs were trembling, her body shaking with desire. He drank from her more, teasing her clit with his tongue and teeth as he held her to him. When she begged him again, telling him that she wasn't able to stand, he stood up and pulled her body to his, lifting her up so that her legs were wrapped round him. He could take her this way if he wanted.

"Mine." She nodded as she wrapped around him higher, her legs tight around his hips, her arms around his shoulders. "Tell me, Kate. Say that you're mine."

"Yours. I belong to no other but you." He took them to the bed then, crawled up it with her tight against his body, his cock aching to be inside of her. He wanted to make this last, make love to her slowly and with reverence, but she was begging him to finish her, to fill her, and he knew that he would do anything she wanted.

Entering her felt like he'd come home…his body, his mind all in line where it felt like they should have been. His cock not only fit inside of her, but seemed to know, too, that there would be no other woman but this one. His body, his heart, all of him filled her now, not just with sexual contact but with heart and soul. He moved in and out of her slowly as she touched him with her mouth and fingers. Her hands danced along his skin, making him more aware of her than he'd ever been of anyone in his life. Every touch of her fingers had him craving more of her. Not just her touch, but all of her.

"I need to taste you." He did her as well. Lifting his head from her ample breast, he looked down at her as he continued to take her, his strokes slow and strong as she pulled his throat to her mouth. "When I bite you, you and I will be one. Forever. All right?"

"We are one now, my Kate. We always have been."

Her words were muffled by her mouth over his pounding pulse. And when she licked him, Chris knew that he was going to come and there would be no holding back. His own teeth shifted in his mouth, his cat making Chris aware that his mate was his as well. As soon as she sank her fangs into his throat, Chris cried out, emptying himself into her even as he bit down on her shoulder to make the connection between them complete.

Nothing could have prepared him for the emotions that came to him. And her memories. He could see them, running through his mind like a fast moving movie. Too fast to make out, but he knew that they were his now, too. When she came again, screaming out his name in his mind, Chris let his own body release, feeling the climax through every cell in his body.

Kate came twice more as they drank from each other. He wanted to come again, his body filling again to do just that, when he felt through their connection that she was close again. Her thoughts were his; her emotions — and there were plenty of them right now — bombarded his. As he lifted his head, he looked at her, watched her face while she came, his body becoming not just hers but a part of them both. Even as he emptied into her again, feeling her tighten around him as she released as well, Chris knew that he was in love with her and would be forever. He knew then that Pella had been nothing at all to him.

Dropping atop her, he felt the pain in his arms. Then his back. He knew what it was…he was being marked again. But when she began to thrash under him, he remembered that she would be marked too, and lifted his body from hers to hold her while the pain took her.

Her screams tore at his heart. Blood covered them both as they were tatted by some unknown force. Wings, he knew, were being formed. Markings would proclaim them as one, and magic that would only be theirs would also be formed. As she continued to be inked, all he could think about was that if he could, he'd take the pain into his own body and bear it for her. Chris held her while she sobbed and told her how sorry he was.

When she fell into a fitful sleep, Chris got up to change the bed linen. As he washed up, keeping an eye on her the whole time, he wondered what had happened to Remy and Skylar. He knew that they too would have gotten some of the markings that he and Kate now had.

As he made his way back into the bedroom, Chris made a sort of observation that the room was different. It was bigger for one thing, and he now had two closets instead of just the one. Even the linens that were forever in plentiful supply in his closet were now doubled, and he thought the towels were a little larger and more plentiful. As he pulled the bloodied sheets off the opposite side of the bed from the one she was on, he thought of other things as well. Like what would happen to his cat now.

Almost as if he'd called for him, his cat stirred along his body. He'd been there his whole life, saving his ass more times than he wanted to admit, so when he stirred, almost becoming a part of his skin, Chris paused in what he was doing and looked around for a mirror. He looked at Kate when she said his name.

"He's there. I see him." Chris nodded, too stunned to think what she meant by that. "I mean, it's like he's a separate part of you, like another being. Don't you think?"

"He feels that way as well. I need to shift." Kate sat up on the bed, pulling the dirty sheet over her when he let his cat take him. Chris knew there was a difference there, too.

"You're beautiful. I never...you are different, like you said. Were you always this big?" She was sitting up now, leaning against the back of the bed and watching him. "I mean, even your coloring is more intense. Like you.... Never mind. I'm being silly."

No. I was larger than a regular panther, but I feel...I feel fucking huge. She laughed and told him he was. *And stronger too.*

When she got up, pulling the sheet around her, he was disappointed but watched her walk to the closet. He was ready to tell her that there wasn't a mirror there, but as soon as she opened the door, he could see one. Moving to it, careful not to knock things over, he looked at the cat staring back at him.

She was right about the colors. His dark coat was a blue black now, shinier than it had been before. He could see small spots of lighter color now where his coat had been simply black before. But it was his face that he took the final steps to see up close.

His eyes were bluer. Not just the blue of what he'd always thought of as a summer sky, but richer. Like the sun was shining on the waters of a large body of water and he was reflecting them back. His muzzle was thicker too, his jawline longer. Opening his mouth, he really wasn't surprised to find his teeth bigger and sharper looking, and there were more of them, it seemed. Turning to look at Kate when she sat near him on the floor, he could put his head over hers, he was that much larger than he'd been before.

Shift for me. Become a cat.

She stood up then, dropping the sheet, and let the animal take her. He had no idea if she was bigger than she'd been before, but he'd bet on it. And like his coat, hers was black as sin and just as thick. Kate rubbed her head to his neck, and he felt his cat approve. Whatever had happened to them when they came together was making them better. But when she moved along his body and up the other side so that they were facing the mirror, Chris only had a few seconds to marvel at how beautiful they looked before dizziness swamped him.

~~~

Remy felt something roll over him, like something had hit him from behind and did it twice more until he could no longer stand. He fell back in the large truck he'd been helping unload when he felt the incredible pain of being marked again. He knew that was what it was; it had happened to him before. He had no idea where it might be going on...as far as he could tell, his body was fully marked as it was. And when Skylar came to him, her body stiff with pain too, he moved as close to her as he could before he dropped to his knees. This time, whatever markings they were getting were more painful than any he'd had before. He tried to sit up twice, but all he managed to do was hurt himself more. Remy couldn't even get to Skylar, and that hurt him more than anything.

After about twenty minutes, he was able to move without his body hurting enough to take his breath away. He was glad now that he'd come out here to burn off some energy and was alone in the big truck. To have someone see him taken to his knees would have been embarrassing to say the least. When he was sitting up, still hurting but not nearly as bad, Skylar came to sit with him. Neither of them said anything for several minutes. He wondered aloud if she'd been marked as well.

"Yes. I feel like I've been run over by this truck. Several times." He told her he did as well. "What the fuck was that? I'm assuming that it has something to do with Chris and Kate, right?"

"Yes. I would...it really hurt this time. I will only admit that to you, but I have never been in so much pain before." The sound of screams had him standing, pulling his sword as he did so when he looked out across the yard to the house. There were children there, none of them in any danger that he could immediately see, but he could tell that something was wrong. Parents were moving toward their offspring at an alarming rate. "Skylar, is there something in the heavens coming after them?"

"No," she laughed. "But I think we just got a new fighting machine by way of the two of them." He looked at her, not understanding her humor, when she pointed to his left. The cat coming toward them was as big as he was. Not just wide, though that was enough, but tall too. He'd bet that on its hind legs it would stand taller than he was. "I think that Chris might be able to take on Benton himself."

"'Tis not just Chris." Skylar asked him what he meant, and he got down from the truck, putting his sword away, and stood in front of the cat. "Kate and Chris, they are this cat, if I don't miss my guess. They have...I would think that they've merged to be one."

The cat, black as the night and as big as a larger car, sat down in front of him. His head now was at Remy's chest, and he was glad that for once something this large was on his side. And when he opened his mouth, the cat seemingly yawning, Remy thanked whatever powers there were that he did not have to stand and be this beast's meal. For it would be a painfully slow death, he'd bet.

"What shall we call you? I'm thinking that you're both there, yes?" Chris answered him that they were, and he had no idea what they were. "You're big, I'll tell you that much. Have you seen yourself?"

No. Just...the mirror wasn't big enough to show us like this. I'm thinking that...if my paws are any indication, we're twice the size I was alone. Remy told him he thought so as well. *Remy, this is some fucked up shit.* He didn't know exactly what that meant, but he thought that Chris had the right of it.

Since I'm an elite shifter, we thought maybe we could see if Chris is as well. We were wondering if we could have you watch us and see if we can change to other animals. As well as merge again.

Remy glanced up when he saw Nate coming toward them. He hadn't been out much since he'd been staying here, and Remy was glad to see him. All of them turned to watch the man as he shifted to a panther, his shift leaving nothing behind as in clothing as he thought should happen.

Nate stared at the cat, his body stiff with something akin to fear, Remy thought. Before Remy could guess his intent, the big cat lay down before the bigger animal. Remy watched with Skylar as Nate rolled to his back and exposed his belly to them. He had no idea what that meant in the animal world.

"He's submitting." He looked over at Rick when he spoke. "The smaller cat, Nate I'm assuming, is submitting to the bigger one. It's the way they would do things in nature. Cats, especially panthers, are a lonely lot, but when they're together, they're called a leap. I'm thinking that whoever this one is, he's got himself a pack now."

"It's Chris and Kate. They're one cat."

Rick laughed. Remy supposed in a way it was funny. But he wondered how they thought of this. When Kate asked again if they could come apart and try another animal, he stopped them when Hector came toward them. The man looked very upset.

Making his way toward him, watching for anything that might be after the older man, Remy thought the man had come in contact with Dolin or Ward, and he hoped that he was all right. Chris, as a man, walked beside him as they closed the distance between them and Hector.

"We keep our clothing, I guess. Or at least we have some when we shift to this form. Who knows what else might happen?" Remy nodded and looked back at Kate, who was coming with them as well. "I don't know what happened. I've been marked again. I know that we both have wings and that...Christ, Remy, this is scary."

"Aye it is, and me too. Along with Skylar." They were standing in front of Hector now, and Remy asked him if he was all right. "You've the look of a man who has seen a ghost. Nothing happened to you there, did it? I didn't want you to go. I think you should have listened to me, yes?"

"I'm fine. It's all fine. I think. Ward and Dolin are both dead. I believe that Benton killed them. And they've been gone for some time, so I'm not sure. Their bodies have been torn apart, spread out in different areas that...it makes me wonder what has happened there. He's insane...Benton has lost his mind. Or what little there was of it when this began. Also, he's looking for people to make a drug for him. I have no idea what it could be, but I mean...I have a drug here that I'm going to have analyzed, but I think it's the only reason that he's still alive."

Ruben came up to his father then and hugged him tightly. The next few minutes were him showing his son things that he'd gotten for him from the other realm. When Ruben walked away, Hector looked like he might have aged several years in the short time he'd been gone.

"The realm is all but dead, Remy, and the little that is still living won't last long, not with him still there. Most has been destroyed beyond whatever wars that we had prior to this. I don't think...there is nothing left."

"I'm sorry."

Hector nodded at him and looked away. There were memories there for the man that he'd never be able to get back. And his wife was buried there as well, Remy only just remembered. Remy asked him what other things he had with him when it looked as if Hector had control of his emotions again.

"Books that I thought we could use here. I managed to get some seeds as well in the store. A few boxes of drugs that I found in the lab before I left. Plants that I could save. Some things for my son, things I could not take when I left before. Snapshots of his mother and things that...that I thought he'd like." He looked back at Remy again, tears in his eyes. "My world is no more. Whatever am I going to do now?"

"Live your life here, with us. Keep your memories alive for your son, the good ones. Try and be brave for him and go on putting your feet forward." Remy nodded at Chris when he spoke up. "Raise your son in a way that your wife would have been proud of. He's a good boy, Ruben, and I think he will give you more than you think you deserve over the next few hundred years. Be happy too. I think that's the most important thing."

"Thank you. Thank you so much, Chris. I can try, but it's so much to bear alone now." Remy told him it would get easier, but not any less painful. "Yes, I can see that now. And I have to admit to you that I now know your pain when I came upon you on that field all those centuries ago. The reason that you wished to die. Of late, it is on my mind a great deal...the disservice that I did to you when all you wished to do was end your life. I am truly sorry for that."

"You have given me more in return, Hector. You must know that. I have friends aplenty. I have a mate that is my equal in all things. I feel...I must admit to you that I feel good about my life now. I miss my wife, yes, and my children, but this life, it has been worth what you did to me." Hector nodded and Remy pulled him into his arms for a great hug. When he returned it, sobbing slightly at his shoulder, Remy held him. He knew the man's pain more than most would have. "You are a good man, Hector. It's a pleasure to call you friend."

They made their way to the boxes and bags of stuff after a few minutes more, and Remy felt like he'd been given a great gift in Hector. Hector said that when he'd made his way to the portal, he'd only had a few things, two boxes and a bag. But he knew that he'd never return, at least he didn't think so, and had gone back for more things. More plants, the pictures, and a few things that he thought that he'd like to see again. When it was all said and done, there were nine large boxes, a crate, and several books, as well as more plants and seedlings that Remy wondered how he'd gotten here.

Hector flushed when he told them how he'd had to send some of the stuff through the portal without him before he'd been able to leave himself. Then he told them what he'd found when he'd entered the lab.

"There are three men there; well, there were three when they came into the lab. I'd been there but only a few minutes when they startled me. I had found it in such a state that for a moment, I forgot to keep aware. Benton killed two of them before I was gone." Remy asked him if he'd been seen by Benton. "Oh no. I was well hidden from them. The men, they had seen me when I was in the area, but they knew not where I was."

Remy took the vial when it was handed to him. He'd seen such things in his lifetime. Mostly in hospitals and such. Lately more in the hands of those that would abuse them, such as drug users and the like. The tip was bent and would more than likely spill its contents out rather than in the intended place. Remy handed it over to Weston when he asked to see it.

"That man, Buddy, he worked in the labs before, so he might be able to figure out how this was made. I've no idea what it might be other than Benton said he needed it as his medication. But if Buddy is going to be reproducing this, whatever it is, for Benton, I'm not sure that's a good idea." Weston asked him if he knew if it might have been something that Randall had taken to make him stronger. "No…I'm sorry, I don't. I'm not even sure it's of this world or what is left of mine. If I need to go back and get some of the ingredients I shall, but my thought was that we could make it here, swapping out one of the drugs for something that might kill Benton, and then perhaps have him die there."

Weston said that he'd give it his best shot, and put it in a small container before looking over the other things that were brought to them. Most of the plants were healthy and in very good shape, but they were a little concerned as to what effect they would have on the plant life in their realm. It was decided that they'd plant them in a controlled area to make sure they didn't sprout wings and come after them. Remy didn't think that was funny, but apparently it had been a joke.

When everything was cataloged and put into other containers, Remy went to find Skylar. Things were too quiet for him. There had not been a call out all day, and as much as he was enjoying the rest, he did not want to get too comfortable with it. So when he found her in the yard with one of the little dogs, he stood watching her while she and the little mutt played. Something that they had not had in some time was fun. When she saw him, he went to her and was handed the little fat fur ball.

"Did you ever have a dog?"

Remy told her that when his children were small, they'd begged for one. He smiled at the memory, glad that it wasn't as painful to remember any longer.

"There was this bitch who had whelped a litter down the road from us. I think his name was Welsh...the man, not the dog. He was glad to get rid of the lot of them before he had to...well, he was glad to get rid of them. Food then was hard to come by, and having a drain, even dogs, wasn't something that he could afford. I took me three of them. My mistress, she fussed at me something powerful, but in the end was glad that I'd done it." Skylar touched the small animal, who was soft as down behind the ears, as he continued. "The children, they were abed when I came home with them, but shot out of their beds like rockets when they heard the pups yipping and going on. No matter what I'd do, they were bound to be found by my children that night, I think. Happy they were to have them."

He realized that his speech was like it had been all that time ago, and watched Skylar as she leaned on his shoulder. His own wife would have smacked him gently on the shoulder should he have told her what he'd traded for the pups. An entire bushel of corn for them had been a great deal back then. But Welsh was a proud man and one that was down on his luck. He could have taken the pups for free, he knew that, but that would not have helped the man and his family. So with little sacrifice to his family, Remy told him that he needed to make a fair trade or his own lady wife would have had his head for him.

"We had them for a year or so. Grand memories of them and the children as the pups grew bigger seemingly by the day. That winter, they tied them to the sled and had them pull them around the yard. The pups—I forget their names—they did it willingly, knowing that my children would love them all the more for it." He didn't tell her that they too had been burned alive by the monsters...not like the ones they fought now, but to his way of thinking worse. He wanted this memory, like so many, not to be tainted by that time. "A robber could have come in and had we had any, the pups would have led them to the best china we had. But the children, they loved them. And it was worth the little that it cost us to have them."

"Remy, when this is done—and I have to believe that it will be someday—would you have children with me?" He looked over at Skylar as she petted the sleeping pup, not looking at him so that he could see if she jested with him or not. "I don't care what we have, boys or girls, but I'd very much like to have your child."

He felt his heart twist up. Not from the pain of trying to replace those that he'd lost so long ago, but with love, his love for Skylar and her wanting to have his child. As he held the puppy gently in his arms, he thought of her fat with his child, her breasts swollen with milk to nurse them, and he knew that he'd like that more than he had anything in a long while.

"I'd like to have many, if you've a mind to. Sons and daughters, as many as you want." She looked at him and he could see her fear there. "You worry too much, my love. We will win this war. I know it. Why, just today we found out that Dolin and Ward are both dead. That will be good for us, I think."

"Every day I see what things have gone on. The amount of people that have been murdered and changed into things that they would never have been." He nodded and pulled her close to him as she cried. "I'm not tender hearted, but so much has been lost that we'll never get back, Remy. What if we can't make this work, even after the malefactors are all gone?"

"When you came into my life that day, I no more wanted you there than I did the responsibility of helping people that no more cared that I was fighting this war than the change they had in their pockets. A war that I thought could not be won. But I saw you fight them that day as if you knew that had you not, then all would have been lost. You tore into them as if you knew you were going to win. And every day I see that same fight in you, and know that we will win." He hugged her tightly to him. "You are the reason that I can do this. The reason that I believe that we will not just be victorious, but that we will bring this world back. And our children will thank us for it."

When the puppy had had enough, he was let go. Skylar moved to sit across his lap and he pulled her close to him. He loved having her there with him, and told her what he'd learned from Hector.

"So they're both dead. I'm glad. One less thing we have to worry about. I talked to Jake a little while ago, and he said that there are only about a quarter of the malefactors that there were last week. He said that he thought that they were no longer being made." She moved her mouth down his neck to his pulse there, and he felt it pick up speed. "He said that he had a thought as to why they had been here and not all over the world."

"Me." He was having a hard time listening to her when she started to unbutton his shirt. "You keep that up and you're going to be flat on your back in no time."

"Yes, you." He had to think what she was saying and nodded when he got it. "But also the proximity to the mountains. He thinks that there was a higher concentration of the agates that they wanted when they came here. It was a double bonus for them. Remy, you have too many clothes on."

He was naked before she bit down on his neck. Then he made sure that she was just as undressed in the next second and rolled her to her back, him between her pretty thighs. When she giggled, he paused in his pursuit of her nipple and looked up at her.

"We're out in the open. Anyone coming by can see us." He willed them to their room and to the bed. It was much softer than the ground anyway. "Oh Remy, whatever did I do to deserve you?"

"You let a man grab your arm and come to me." He kissed her nipple as he made his way down her body. "Now hush, woman, I need to feast upon your body. And then when I am done, I will make sure that I did not miss anything whilst I was at it."

He ate her like a man possessed. Her breasts, her pussy. Remy even tasted her knees and ankles. Her elbows tasted of cranberries, the lotion he knew that she put on nightly. Her ears the same, with a little hint of sexual appeal. Her nipples, hard and a dusky rose, perked up for him, tightened as he nibbled in them none too gently. Every time she came so nicely for him, he gave her just a little more of himself. Remy was on a mission...a mission to show his lady wife just how much he loved her. And he didn't want her to think him remiss in giving her as much pleasure as he could.

When she came again, this time screaming loud enough to make him laugh, he moved up her body until his cock was at her entrance. She was wet, her body ready for his, but he paused. The look in her eyes at that moment said to him more than mere words could ever tell him. Skylar loved him.

"I do too."

He moved into her gently, filling her rather than just fucking her. When she wrapped her legs around him, pulling his body tighter to her own, Remy felt each ripple of her sheath, every nuance of her as he made love to her properly. And when he bit her, taking another part of her into him, she sank her own teeth into him and he released as he felt a man should when he had the love of his life.

Chapter 6

Buddy read the notes again. He was sure that these were the wrong doses, but with Benton standing over him, smelling like rotted flesh, he wasn't sure what he was doing. Buddy stretched his neck again, feeling the tension lighten just a little in the sound of a pop.

"You have it?" He didn't and told Benton that. He'd also taken it upon himself to tell Benton that he needed him to back off and stop scaring the shit out of him all the time. The monster had been threatening him almost every ten minutes since yesterday morning. "What is it you need from me? I am running low on supplies."

"I don't know what I need. I'm just trying to find what works for you." He looked at the thing in front of him. "I'm working on notes of things that have failed. Not things that worked. I have to start fresh every time one fails. And when it does, you make me...you have to stop treating me like someone who is trying to cheat you. I have to see what he failed at so that I do not fail too. And you standing there, asking me every time I pick up something if I have it, is fucking not helping."

Benton's temper flared, and Buddy hoped that the conversation he'd had with him just yesterday had helped with that as well. There was no one here to help him. If he killed Buddy, he was never going to get what he wanted. And at this point, Buddy would almost welcome death over this. This constant bombardment of demands. The threat of being killed almost every minute. He was too nervous to fail, yet did at every turn because he was so terrified.

"What shall I do for you then?" Buddy wanted to tell him to leave him alone and let him go back into hiding, but that wasn't going to work. He was stuck here, at least until he was no longer useful to Benton. And even then Buddy wasn't sure that he was going to be able to leave. Not on his own, at any rate. "You say you need space. I have nothing to do to keep me from badgering you. What do you need for me to do?"

"Clean this place up. The bodies have to go. I can't...and take a bath, please." He wanted to laugh it off, but Benton really did smell. "I need to work in an environment that isn't making me sick to my stomach." Benton looked like he was going to lash out at him again, and Buddy backed away. The last time he'd lost his temper, Buddy had had to put ten stitches in his arm. He was really afraid of the creature and his temper.

"I do not do manual labor. I am Master. And as such, I will not stoop to picking up the dead and disposing of them for you." Buddy bent his head over the table that he was working on and tried to ignore him. "But I do have an idea how to help you. I do not smell well, and this room is filled with things that are unhealthy to me. It is my opinion that I need to clean this area up, then bathe. A nice soak in a tub will do me a world of good, I think."

Whatever worked for him. Buddy had noticed that it had to be Benton's idea when it came to things. Not just the work area, like now, but with everything. When Buddy had suggested that power be turned back on to the labs, Benton had told him no. Then ten minutes later, the power came on and Benton—or Master, as Buddy was told to call him— had said that he'd realized that power would make things better. That he could not see with the lights off. Then he'd scolded Buddy like one would a small child for not telling him sooner that he needed lights to work. He also said that Ward and Dolin had thought it was a good idea as well.

That was something else that had creeped him out a little…the way that Master had continued to talk to the two dead men. And Buddy was sure that both of them were dead. Their bodies, or at least parts of them, had turned up when he'd been trying to clear a space to work in. But almost every conversation that he had with Master had been talked over with either of the two dead men. And then there was Mary.

Buddy remembered Mary. Everyone had thought her to be so saintly and kind hearted, but he knew her to be a conniving and mean spirited woman. When she didn't get her way, she would pout for days on end. And if things did not turn out the way she wanted, she would lash out at the person she thought she could hurt. Mary played the two men, Ward and Dolin, every time she spoke to the other. She would manipulate them into doing things that neither man, Buddy thought, would have ever thought of on their own. But now, she, too, was here in the room with him. Ordering him about as if she were still alive and he was beneath her.

He looked at Master when he said his name. "You will have me something in the morning. I don't care should it not work right away, but I am running low on my medicine. And anything that you make will have to be ready to help me. Do you understand me?"

"I do, but you have to know that I'm doing my best with what I have to work with. There are no test subjects here, so I have to wait to see if anything works the way you want it to when you come back. And you being here all the time doesn't work either." He'd hoped the man would let him go and find him someone he could use the drugs on, and Buddy would simply not return. "I can go and get someone. I know where a few of the others are hiding out."

The low growl was all the warning he got before Buddy had to leap back out of the way of the claws that seemed to come out of nowhere. His body slammed against the wall and he saw stars, but didn't move to get up. The monster was back, it seemed, and Buddy hoped again that he was going to kill him.

"I need the medicine now. No more making demands of me. I am Master." The thing grew and grew, knocking over the tables that had only just been set up again. Buddy's notes, too, were scattered all over the room, and he knew this was going to be the end. And in a sad way, he was hoping that it was. Working like this was going to kill him anyway. He turned his head away from Master and waited for the final blow.

The silence kept him there. Master was waiting, Buddy knew, for him to turn and then would kill him. It was perhaps five minutes before he'd finally had enough and turned with one eye open, trying to see without alerting Master. He was alone in the room.

Standing up quietly, hoping not to be lured into some sort of trap this way, Buddy looked around the room again. Yes, he was alone. For now anyway. And as suddenly as he realized that, he knew what was wrong with the formula he'd been working on. Going back to where he'd been working, his head buzzing with the way it had to work, he cleaned up the mess left behind by Master's temper and set to work. Finding the chemicals needed to work with proved to be much harder than he'd hoped, but soon he had them all and started measuring them out.

Buddy had no idea what time it might have been when Master returned. It was late, he knew that, and he was hungry. But excited too. He'd made a large batch of what he knew was going to work, hoping that once Master saw how busy he'd been, he'd have to let him go. It was a long shot, but Buddy felt too good about things right now to worry too much. He turned to the man, excited, and took a step back. Master had someone with him.

"I found you a test subject. I thought that perhaps you could use one to try out the drugs you make on him before I take them." Buddy nodded, never taking his eyes from the man that was held in his claws. He'd been beaten up...his lip was swollen, as was his eye. There was blood on his chest as well, deep red, so Buddy knew that it was fresh. Even Master looked as if he'd had a time of it with the man. His body looked a little worse for wear, too. "You will test the drugs on him when you make them. If it will enhance him, then I shall take it. I think that is the best way, do you not agree?"

"What if it kills him?" Master growled and tossed the big man at him. Picking him up again, Master shoved him into the cage that had until recently held the body of two dead, decomposing men. Buddy said nothing as the man lay there, not even fighting for his freedom. He must have been hurt badly was all he could think about.

Buddy wanted to tell him that he had it, that there was no need for him to have the man here. But he was also afraid that Master would kill him, the stranger, and for some reason, Buddy knew that to do that would bring a world of hurt down on him that he'd never survive. He picked up the filled needle and made his way to the man.

"Your name?" The man only stared at him. Buddy was afraid that if he gave this powerful man this drug that he might escape and kill him for it. Better to cover his own butt than to end up stacked in the corner with the rest of the dead. "I'm Buddy. Your name? I can maybe help you if you let me."

"And how would you do that? Let me go? Change me back to what I was before all this shit happened?" The laughter was bitter and harsh. "Yeah, I'm so trusting of that too. But know this...if you give me that shit and it works, you're going to be the first thing I kill when I get out of here. And hear me when I tell you, I will fucking get out of here."

Master roared out and the man in the cage only stood there. Buddy was cowering back, not wanting to be anywhere near Master or the man when things got worse than they were. And he had no doubt that they would. But when he was ordered to inject the drug into the tatted man, Buddy told him he was sorry.

No one moved but Buddy. And he only moved back as far from the cage as he could go. The man, whoever he was, just stood there, his body hard against the bars of the cage. But when the drug started to work, Buddy wasn't sure if he wanted to jump for joy or run and hide. It did just what they had hoped it would be.

He grew. Not just his muscles, as Master had told him he wanted, but his height and girth as well. The cage, big enough for several men his size, was suddenly too small for him, his body no longer pressing against the bars but making the metal bulge and the hinges weaken. Buddy backed up more. He knew that when the doors came free, the man was going to come for him. And Buddy wanted nothing to do with it. Master turned to him before the transformation of the tatted man was complete.

"You will make more." Buddy nodded, not taking his eyes off the cage. It was close now; soon it would be like the rest of the rubble in the room. "Give me the rest. And you'll make more. Now."

Buddy pointed to the table where the large container was that he'd made up. He'd meant to tell him to take it in small doses, that he'd made the strength stronger than Master had asked him for. But it was too late. For a lot of things, Buddy thought. Master picked it up and drank it down. Buddy knew a new kind of fear then. Master was changing, and not for the good.

~~~

"I've not seen him for hours, and I've asked around…no one else has either. Not that anyone sees him all that much anyway, but he's not on the compound." Davis tried not to worry. It really wasn't his job to keep track of a full grown man that didn't want to be a part of anything, but there had been sightings of Benton, and he worried that Nate would go to him just to spite them all. "You checked his room?" he asked Vicki again.

"Yes, I've checked his room." He could tell that Vicki was getting worried too. Her tone told him that, or else she was mad at him. He wanted to believe it was Nate. "Did you ask Skylar to help? Or Kate? She has some pretty freaky abilities."

So did Vicki, but he didn't point that out. They had called to the earth and there had been no help there either. Nate was simply gone. Not just not on the compound where they could find him, but he didn't seem to be touching the earth anywhere.

Davis put a call out to Remy and Skylar when the two of them had looked everywhere they could think of for Nate. They were both on a call, something about a warehouse that they owned that was being invaded, and while he'd heard it wasn't that bad, they still had left. He thought they were glad to get away...it was simply too quiet here for his tastes as well. Davis had always been the type that knew that the other shoe was going to drop. And when it did, there was going to be hell to pay.

You sure that he was there earlier? Davis told Skylar that he was, that he'd been his usual friendly self at breakfast. *He's going to have to either get his shit together or get out. I've had enough of this crap. And if he's packed his bags and left, I swear to you I'm going to cut his balls off and serve them up to him.*

Most of the others were sick of him as well. Nate never helped them. They weren't even sure that he was eating well. Just the other morning he'd been in the dining hall when Davis and Vicki had entered, and he had gotten up and left the cup of tea on the table cold. Things were out of control with him, that was for sure.

Benton has been around too. One of the others saw him a few hours ago near the cave up on the west side of the compound. And that building downtown, no matter what we do to keep people out, they seem to be drawn to it. You think that it has some magical draw that is pulling people to it? Skylar said she had no idea, but that they'd done enough now that it was time to destroy the stupid thing. Remy said he was going to do it tonight. *Thank goodness.*

I've a mind to go through it, just to see what's on the other side.

Davis thought of something while Remy talked about what he had in mind if it was some sort of portal to the other side. *Nate said that. I don't...we were in the family room and Chris mentioned the building. Just offhandedly, Nate said something about testing the boundaries of it. Do you suppose he's gone there?* Christ, Davis hoped not. There wasn't any way for them to help him should he have gone there. *Has anyone checked the footage that we have on the place?*

Davis was on his way to the command center as he spoke. Whatever happened there, they had recordings of it. It looped around every six days, so he knew that if Nate had gone there, they'd know it. He asked Jake to pull it up while Davis continued to speak to Remy and Skylar.

In less than fifteen minutes they had their answer. Nate hadn't gone through the building. Not on his own anyway. He'd been standing just on the outside of it, a few feet away, when Benton appeared. He had snatched him up at that point and taken him through the doorway to the beyond.

Skylar and Remy were on their way to the building as soon as they saw what had happened. Chris and Kate entered the command center just as Davis was getting ready to leave as well. They were all going, it appeared, to see what they could do about bringing Nate back.

He'd driven. While Davis didn't mind his wings most of the time, he was still having some trouble landing. Nearly every time, his feet would get all tangled up and he'd end up on his ass. Or worse, knocking someone else down as soon as he tumbled. He was getting out more, practicing as much as he could, but lately, he'd been having too much fun with his new mate.

"Now what?"

No one seemed to have a clue as they stood at the point where Nate had been taken. If they went into the building, no one had any idea if they would come back. Remy asked who was going with him. Rick and Hector stopped him just as the big man was ready to go charging through.

"I would like to go first." Remy was shaking his head even before Rick finished. "Listen to me for a minute. Whatever is on the other side of this can't be any worse than what we have here. If I die, what are you out? Nothing. I have no mate to leave behind pining for me, nor do I have much in the way of money. I mean, I have some, but I've been investing in things. By the way, cool way to get paid."

"Be that as it may, I should go first. I know the area better than anyone." Davis thought that Hector had a good point, but he also had a son that would need him. And if anything happened to Hector...well, Davis thought the boy had lost enough for one small lifetime. Skylar pointed that out to him. "I know that he's in good hands should something happen."

"I'm going." Everyone turned to Chris. "I mean, Kate and I are going. We are the biggest of us all when we're together. And we can pretty much whip Benton's ass long enough for Nate to be found and him get back to us. I mean, the guy is a pain in the ass, but he's our family whether he likes us or not."

"Nay, that will not work. What if he is too hurt to come on his own? I like that you can fight together, but I think there needs to be more." Skylar nodded and smiled at them all. Remy winced. "I don't like that look, love. What is it you have in mind?"

"We all go. But Hector." When he started to protest, she put up her hand. "Listen to me first. You said you know the place better than us. Right, you do. So if we don't come back quickly, you can come there and get us. You can do that whole invisibility thing and be in and out before Benton is the wiser, making sure that we're back here in time for dinner tonight. And besides, someone needs to be here in the event that one of us needs to be taken to the medical unit."

"But I could go in and snoop things out." Skylar corrected him and told him that he'd try to rescue the man and he knew it. "Yes, I would. But I should also like to point out that I am very good at scoping things out. I did tell you that Dolin and Ward were dead."

"You did at that. And that really is valuable information. But we need you here. If you're here, all of us will be safer in the event you have to come and get us." Davis thought that was a load of shit, but only nodded when Hector looked at them. The man really was a valuable asset, but only in the sense that he knew things about the creatures that were coming for them. He wasn't good at fighting, nor did he have any abilities that would give him an edge over Benton. Skylar looked hard, her body tense with some kind of anger. "I'm going to need you here, Hector. I know that I'll feel better just knowing that someone is on this side to help us if we need it. And that someone is you."

"I think you give me much more credit than I deserve, but I see your point. And I don't like it, but I see you are set on it happening this way." He told them how to get to the lab, and like a GPS, told them precisely when they had to turn and what the kilometers were they had to walk. Davis did better with feet and miles, but he knew that at least a few of them knew where they were going.

"We go in all at once. If anyone is left behind, we go on. It might only take a few at a time, so we move as a unit until we figure this out." Davis held Vicki's hand as Remy told them what to do. He'd be insane with worry should he go or stay and not be with her. He was sure that the rest of them would with their own mates as well. "Once there, we do nothing more than go to the lab and get Nate. If he's not there, we regroup where we land on the other side."

"Weapons? Will they go with us?" Everyone turned to Hector at Leo's question, and he said that only the things on their bodies could go. "All right. So that means that we're armed with just what art we have on our body. Which, to my way of thinking, is better than nothing, right?"

Good point. Davis had forgotten about the tats that actually came for them to use. He had a sword and several guns. So did Vicki. He also knew that while they could be dragons, both Leo and Jamey were armed as well. Skylar and Remy had more than the rest of them in the way of tats, but he wasn't sure other than the swords what other weaponry they had on them. In other words, he thought them as well equipped as they could be, yet not at all. Who knew what they were going to face on the other side?

As one they moved through the break in the building. Davis closed his eyes, not wanting to be looking down the throat of death when he landed, or however it happened on the other side, and nearly wet his pants when someone screamed. He opened his eyes to see three woman standing by a waterway washing their clothing.

It was...normal, he supposed. They'd been sitting there, a picnic basket between them, with what looked like greens and bottled water. Their laundry, not really much of it, was in the water or laying out on the grass to dry. He thought about taking a picture, and realized that he'd not had a camera nor a phone for longer than he could remember being without them before. He tipped an imaginary hat at them both when they continued to stare at them.

"You come from the other realm? Just so's you know, you scared ten years off my life with you just appearing like that. Don't do it again." No one said a word, but they must have guessed the answer. "You here for that monster? If so, he's in the caves above us. We come here to do the washing when he's there. Spends his nights there too, most times. If you have it in your minds to kill him, I don't think it'll be all that easy."

Remy asked them what he was doing there. The older woman, she didn't gather her things like the younger two. He could feel her sorrow from where he stood as one of the younger women spoke up. Davis noticed that none of them looked at the older woman while she continued at her task.

"He's bringing the others back with him. All sorts of monsters...well, more monstrous than he is—down here to pick over the dead. Some of them creatures, they've been gone longer than I've been here. Most of them just pick the bodies, or whatever they can find, clean, then move on. Couple of them, they got trapped up in that thing over there. Where you come from. You see them?" Skylar asked them how many were left. "Not many. A couple more, but they already moved on. Three men—they worked in the lab—they usually come looking for a handout and we hide from them, but we haven't seen them in a bit. I'm thinking one of them works for that monster, but the others, I think they're dead now...or I hope so. They're not nice and they steal from us. Heard the monster has a terrible temper. By the way, have you seen Hector there? In that other world?"

"He's living in our compound. His son too." The woman nodded at Vicki as if she might have already known that as she continued with gathering her wash. "We can take you back with us should you like to go."

Not bothering to answer, the two of them took off. Davis watched them, not wholly trusting them, but also wanted to make sure that they made it to wherever they were going all right. Skylar made the same offer to the older woman.

"I can't go, but I thank you. My husband is buried over there with my three sons. Murdered by the same monster that has killed our world." She didn't pause in her washing to continue her answer. "I've dug me a nice hole there. Should I be killed too, I'm going to try my best to make it to them, to lay to rest where they are. We don't normally bury our dead. Never did it before, actually, but I figured if I were to light a fire to take care of them, the monster would know I was about. It's...I was gonna say safer, but I don't think any of us would be safe from that. Do you?"

"I'm sorry." Skylar put her hand on the woman's shoulder when grief bent her over. "I'm so sorry for your loss. If I could help you, I want you to know that I would."

"You make sure that you take care of that thing...that is how you can help me. I know that you had nothing to do with that thing and what he's become, but I would like it if I could rest in peace knowing that he's dead and gone. He's done enough here that there won't be nothing left as it is now. Even the ones that come here now, they don't stay long. Scared they are." Remy asked her why there were others coming here and how. "Don't know the how. But they come for the stones they were promised. It's a powerful thing I guess, to some. Not to me. We had enough here, and because of the greed of a few, we've lost it all."

Before they left her and the others, she told them there was a big bell nearby. That if the monster came out too soon for them, before they left, she'd ring it to let them know. Then she asked them to please put her in the hole should she be killed like the others.

"They're all I had in the world, those boys and my husband. All I had. And now they're gone and dead. That monster up there, he don't care one fig what he's done so long as he gets what he thinks is his." Remy asked her if she'd be all right. "No. Not ever again. But you promise me, you make me a promise that you'll try to kill it, and if need be you put me in that soft dirt over there so I can rest with my boys."

"I promise you that we'll do that. But you be careful, please. We might have use for you again should we come this way." She told him that she was too tired now, that she was done in. Remy promised her that if it came to it, they'd make sure she was near her family.

"He's bigger." As they started away, Sally, the woman that had been talking to them, spoke again. "The monster. Don't know what is going on with that, but he's a great deal bigger than he was before. Stupider too, if that was possible. You might want to be a little more careful in dealing with him. He's meaner too. Destroying things as he moves by them, talking about how he is master of all that he can see."

As they made their way to the labs, the path riddled with the dead, all Davis could think about was the time that Benton had come to them as his monster and how big he'd been then. If he was bigger—and he didn't doubt that Sally was telling them the truth—then what were they going to do if he should come back while they were there? He hoped to Christ that they got some sort of warning before he came upon them. He wanted to tell his love that he was glad to have her in his life, and that he loved her with all his heart.

The lab looked like an oversized house...a house that had been hit by a bomb, but a house all the same. The front entrance was broken out, the doors laying on the steps leading to the front of it. Large crocks of flowers, most of them broken, were on each step, the contrast funny to him. Windows were gone, shattered against some unknown force. Davis thought for sure it was Benton, but he knew that a little of it might have been Randall as well. He glanced over at Vicki and wondered if she was thinking about her brother too.

He's gone. He nodded at her voice in his head, and he felt her sorrow. *I think about him here, living with these people and hurting them. But I don't think of him as my step brother any more. He was just a horrible person that took advantage of us. He's gone. Like the people he killed, gone forever.*

I love you. She smiled at him just as they were to enter the building. *You be careful in here. I cannot lose you. Not now.*

And you be careful as well. I don't want to have to beat your ass because you managed to get hurt. Again. He kissed her on the nose and she smiled. Davis was pretty sure he could go for days on just that smile. They entered the building as they had this world, as a unit. Davis had never been as glad for these people in his life as he was right now.

Chapter 7

Kate had been in labs before. At one point in her life, she'd been an assistant to some famous, but now gone, people. But this lab was nothing like anything she'd ever seen before. And she was reasonably sure that no one else had either. This was well beyond state of the art…there were pieces of equipment here that she was sure they had no name for. The sound from across the room had her turning with her hands up, her magic dancing at the tips of her fingers.

"Don't hurt me." The man—or what was left of him— lay in a pool of his own blood. Part of his leg was missing, and it looked as if he'd landed on something that now protruded bloodily out of his belly. "I guess don't hurt me is not what I meant. Could you just finish me off?"

Laughter burbled from his mouth, blood as well. As he moved his arm, his fingers missing too, he wiped at it. Kate wanted to tell him that he'd be all right, but it wasn't in her nature to lie to someone.

"Who are you?" He told her. "Did the creature do this to you, Buddy? He took a friend of ours. Do you happened to know if he was brought here? Or maybe someplace else?"

"He's a monster. That thing, he's a fucking monster." The laughter brought up large amounts of blood from his mouth and wound again. "He ordered me to duplicate this drug. I worked on it with the understanding that he'd let me go. I was sure, somewhere in the back of my mind, that he wasn't going to, but one can hope, right?"

Kate looked around the room, wondering again what some of the busted and broken equipment might have been. But there were no signs of Nate, nor the drug that this man said he was supposed to be working on.

"What was it supposed to do for him?" Kate stood near Chris when he asked Buddy. "And what is the formula for it? Do you have it?"

"Gone. He drank it all down. And yes, the formula is written down, but I don't think I can get up and get it for you. I'm a might indisposed in the event you didn't see that." Again the burble of laughter that brought up copious amounts of blood. "It changed him. I think for good. At least that's what it looked like when he left here. He said that I had given him the greatest gift of all, that when he returned from getting someone by the name of Rembrandt, he would reward me. I just want to end this life."

"There was another man brought here. Do you know where he is?" Buddy pointed, but not well; it was a general direction sort of wave that both frustrated and scared Kate. It meant that Nate had been in this room when all this had happened. "Do you know why he was brought here? What was done to him?"

"He made me." Remy asked him who had made him do what. "Master. I was to call him Master. He made me give that tatted man the drug first. A test subject, he called him. I don't think the man faired any better than I did. He was in the cage when Master went a little over the deep end."

The bell sounded. It rang like there was a hurricane of winds pressing against it, it was so loud and continuous. Everyone in the room froze. But the mewing sound, like that of a soft kitten, had them all turning to the wall and start tossing away scraps of what was left of the lab. They found Nate just as the sound of the bell was cut off.

"Kill me." Remy told Nate that he could not. "Please. Kill me now. I don't know what they did to me, but I can feel it moving under my skin. I think they poisoned me. Please, just kill me now."

"You'll come back with us. Maybe we can take care of you there." Remy picked Nate up, his screaming tearing through Kate's heart even as Leo told them to get out. Remy looked at Leo and told him to take care of it. Even as they were running out of the lab, Nate still screaming to be killed in Remy's arms, Kate could feel the heat. Leo and Jamey were burning the building down with their dragons. Kate was afraid it was too little too late for the realm.

They could see the monster as he came after them. He was big, bigger than houses that he destroyed in his haste, but he was also clumsier, falling every few feet only to get up and try again. If he got to them, even one of them, they would all be killed, for Kate knew that none of them would leave any of the others here should they be attacked. This creature looked as if he was exactly what they thought of him as. A Monster.

They ran as if the devil himself was after them. In a way, Kate was sure that he was. All of them running for a different, but no less important, reason. One of them bent on killing them, the others running to safety. Even in their haste, she noticed that each of them were careful of their surroundings and that they kept together, to keep each of them safe.

Then she came upon the woman, Sally. Her body was broken. There were no other words to describe how she'd been killed. The bell handle was still gripped in her bloodied hand, her eyes wide open in fear and pain. The bell itself was several hundred feet away, still on the wooden structure that it had been mounted on.

Kate was going to fulfill her promise to the woman who had more than likely given her life to warn them that danger was coming. Picking up her body, no one moved beyond circling her as she moved to where Sally had told them she had dug her hole.

"We must hurry." She thought that Skylar was telling her to forget it, to leave the body, that Sally would never know, but she continued. "We'll take her there, but we must hurry. Benton is coming toward us now."

The hole was just where she'd said it would be. There were four more, each of them covered in a pretty blanket of flowers and crudely made markers that proclaimed who was buried beneath them. Putting Sally into the hole, she heard Benton screaming at them, his long strides eating up the distance between them and him. It was still miles yet, but with his size he was closing quickly. They all watched the earth seem to welcome Sally into her depths and cover her up. Kate was sure that like with her magic, Sally had asked the earth when the time came to help her with this one last task, and it had.

Vicki took the blanket, shook it out, and laid it gently over the small mound of dirt. Flowers immediately began to sprout and grow over the other graves as well as Sally's. They picked up their fallen man and each of them took off at a pace that frightened her a little. Speed was necessary, but they were nearly blurred with it. Then Remy took to the skies, and Nate with him. Kate looked at Chris, and they came together to be their beast.

Strength powered over them. Benton paused in his haste to get to them, and she knew that they'd frightened him. Vicki raised her hands, Davis at her back, and white magic as pure as the clouds above them danced from the tips of her fingers. Benton only just managed to leap out of the full stream of it, screaming as it tore at his leg as she and Chris leapt at him.

"Be gone with you." Kate and Chris jumped on Benton again and again, tearing at him even as he hit out at the flames still smoldering on his leg. "Why will you not die? Where is Rembrandt? This is all his fault, he should have died all those years ago. Ward? Help me. You said you'd help me kill them. Where is Rembrandt, and why is he not dead? Ward?"

"Ward is dead and I am here, you fool." Remy landed not five feet from the creature as Chris and she jumped at Benton again. When he only batted them away, standing up to go after Remy, they stood back, ready to protect him if necessary. "You will regret taking one of mine."

"Yours? You think you're master of something? You are not. I am master, and you are to be dead. I will kill you, Rembrandt. Soon too." Benton moved forward, but crumbled when he put weight on his injured leg. Remy stood his ground as he lifted himself from the earth to be eye to eye with the monster. "I will be master; I am the greatest man alive."

Davis was carrying Vicki away. Kate knew that with such powers as hers, she would need to rest. As he made his way to the portal, she and Chris stood by Remy and Skylar. The four of them might not be able to kill the monster, but they would be able to hurt him a great deal.

"You are nothing. Not even a very good monster. Do you think you scare me? Any of us?"

Benton lashed out at Remy, who was able to avoid the contact. When someone touched their fur, they turned to look at Skylar, just narrowly catching themselves before attacking her.

"Go to the portal with the others. Leave the doorway open. Once we are finished here, we will follow." Chris asked her if she was going to kill Benton. "I don't think we can this time. But we will regroup. Remy is just going to distract him so we can get away. Go, be safe."

Chris and she separated, their bodies becoming their own. Kate wasn't sure that they could move any faster, but as they took off, her wings spread from her body, larger than before and stronger. She knew that these wings were because of her mating with Chris. Chris was in flight, too, when they both moved to the gate to go home. Vicki and Davis were just going in as they landed, and the four of them went in together. Vicki was drained, as was Davis, and she worried for them both.

They stood outside the building for an hour, hoping and praying that Remy and Skylar would come through soon. Kate was ready to go back, see what they could find out, when they were suddenly there. In their arms were two men, both of them looking as if they had not eaten in a long while.

"These men will need help. They were at the opening when we got there." Chris took one man, she the other. Vicki and Davis had taken Nate back to the compound.

Skylar collapsed in Remy's arms. Leo and Jamey were waiting to destroy the opening once everyone was through. Remy nodded at their plan. "He lives still, but we have harmed him a great deal. I think...we will need to plan better, I think. He is much stronger than he had been, his body harder to hurt. Whatever he had, it has done him better than we could have ever thought."

"You mean that he might not be able to be stopped." Kate looked around when no one answered her. "You don't mean that, do you? That we can't kill him? That we're going to be fighting this war forever?"

"Nay, I did not say that. But it will not be easy to bring him down." Remy looked around, then back at her. "These creatures, the winged ones from before when we first saw you, you killed them with just a wave of your hand. Are you willing now to tell us what you might be?"

No, she wasn't ready for that. Chris, she was sure, knew, but there was more to her than what they needed to be aware of. But as she was standing there, trying her best to figure out how not to tell them, Cobb came out of the building next to them.

"My lady, you will need to share with them. What you are is going to help them." Remy cleared his throat and Cobb turned to him with a small bow. "She is stronger than you have yet to realize, sir. And now that she has a mate, her true mate, there will be more power. But she must be protected too. For what she is cannot ever be replaced."

"More? More what?" Cobb only looked at her instead of answering Remy. Instead of answering him or Cobb, she went to the car and put the man she was holding in it before turning to them. "I should very much like to know, Kate. I think that it will be helpful to us all to know that we have strength in our numbers."

"I can tell you, but I have to go away for a little while. I'll return, but I must leave for a time. It's part of what I am." Remy started to speak, but she cut him off. "I have things that will help with what we're doing. Information really. Chris can...he may stay or not, but I will return."

"I'm going with you." Kate nodded at Chris, knowing that he would. "Where might we be going? Or are we flying there? Because I have to tell you, that was the only way we got out with our asses, don't you think?" No one answered him, and he turned to Remy as Chris answered his own question. "I would imagine that it is part of what we are. That once we have found the other half of us, then we become more and whole." Remy nodded. "I'll say this again, this is some fucked up shit going on here."

Kate couldn't have agreed more. But in order to tell them what she was, she needed to explain it to Chris. He should know before she tried to tell the others what they both were now. Chris's life, as he'd known it, was about to change. As hers had when she came together with him.

"I have information on what you are as well," she told Remy. "You are not human, as I'm sure you have guessed, but you and Skylar are all."

"All what?" She wasn't sure how to answer that, so she opened her arms wide and let them see her for what she was. A bright light in an otherwise dark world. "Christ. You're magic, pure magic, aren't you? You're the...we've heard about you. Through others, we've heard about a magical creature that would one day come here."

"I am. But the others, they would not have known that I would be helping you in this. They would...I think they would think I was there to destroy you all. I am not." Pulling her magic around her, she looked at Skylar. "You are like me as well, but not as much. On some levels you are stronger, but for the most part, I am the strongest being there is."

"And you're on our side." It wasn't a question, but Kate told her that she was. "Good, because while I have no idea how I'd kill you, you can bet your ass that I would give it my best if you weren't."

"We have to get these men to safety." She nodded at Leo when he spoke, and moved back from the vehicle when he came nearer to her. "I won't harm you."

"You can't. But I can you. Your dragon...he is part of a larger being...Bob, you called him." Leo nodded. "It wasn't until I saw you in the lab that I realized that. He is inside of you and Jamey even now. And when you're together, he protects you even though he cannot be seen."

"Yes. He said that he would be a part of us forever. What else? What else are you not telling us?" She shook her head and told Leo she'd return with answers. "Why do I get the feeling that you're going to create more questions than you can answer for us?"

Remy spoke before she could tell Leo he might not want all the answers he'd be given. "All right, but I want the two of you to be careful out there. No taking chances that you might get hurt doing. All right?"

"We'll be safe. But you won't want to know some of this." He said that more than likely he would not. "We will both return in two days."

~~~

Chris moved along side of Kate, still trying to get used to his wings. They were huge, and he felt like...he really wasn't sure what they felt like, but a part of him was about all he could think of. But the view now that he was in charge of his speed and altitude was amazing.

"They are a part of you. If you think of them as an extension of your arms or body, you can use them better." Chris nodded, and realized that Kate seemed to have a better handle on these than the rest did when they first got them. And come to think of it, so did he. "I've been able to fly for decades, and that knowledge would have been passed to you. I am an elite shifter, so have been able to become an animal that flies for some time. You are also one now, as well as everything that I am. You'll get used to them."

"We never tested the theory that we could be other animals together." She said nothing as they moved along the sky. He looked around, trying to put to his mind that he was several hundred feet in the air and he had no idea where they were headed. "Kate, what is it that you are?"

"We are magic, as Skylar said, but more than that. We are vampire, shifter...really, we are anything we want to be." He asked her what that meant. "When we land, I'll be better able to explain it to you. For now, why not enjoy the freedom we have?"

Nodding, he looked down. It took him several minutes to figure out what his eyes were telling him. There were people, yes, but they were...they were going about their day as normal people might. Not running for cover as everyone he knew did.

Children were in yards playing, and several adults were washing their cars. One woman was even bringing groceries into her home a few bags at a time. He nearly left the sky to go and see what sort of magic this was, and whether he was in some sort of surreal dream.

"They are real. We're far enough away from the compound that you can see that life has gone on without you…or I suppose in spite of you. There were malefactors here, but not nearly as many as you have had. I think, as Remy said, that they were made to go after him. And the things that the mountains can give the other realm." He watched as two children ran around their back yard chasing a puppy. He asked her why these people seemed unaffected by the monsters. "I'm going to show you something."

As they took to the ground, he felt the air around him. It was…while cleaner wasn't really the word, it was the best he could do with what he was smelling. When he asked Kate what he was smelling she laughed at him. She told him he could smell everything now.

He inhaled deeply and looked at her again. "I smell cut grass. Apples with cinnamon. Someone burning leaves, and the sweat of someone working out." She nodded as they moved to a smallish building. "Paint. I smell fresh paint, like someone is painting their home. Gasoline. Why am I smelling these now when we have all of that back at the compound?"

"No, you don't. You have cut grass, but there are no mowers doing it. It just needs to be shorter, so the magic accommodates it. No one has painted your rooms or buildings. When they are in need of repair, the magic knows it and takes care of it. There are no fruit trees on the property, yet you have fresh fruit when desired. The gardens that you have there, I bet there are no weeds in them, and the produce and vegetables are pulled from the ground that is soft and yielding. And the more of you that become whole, the stronger that magic is that takes care of you." He asked her how that was possible. "Remy and Skylar do it."

"I think we might have noticed one or both of them standing in the yards doing these things." Kate just stared at him as they stood by the building. "They don't do it physically, do they? That's not what you meant. It is as much a part of what they are as we are. Magic."

"Yes." She put her hand on the wood and asked him to do the same. "When you come here alone, you will need to show the door who you are. Should you try to open the door without that, it will kill you."

"Kill me how?" He watched as the door just disappeared. When he asked Kate again, he realized that he knew the answer to that as well. "It will remove my head. Then burn my body."

Nodding, she entered the building and he followed. But as soon as he did, Chris had the urge to turn and run. This was no ordinary shed that they were in. It was fucking crazy.

First of all, it was huge. Not like seeming big because there was nothing in it, so it was deceptively larger. No, it was fucking huge. And far from empty. And the deeper he moved into the building, the bigger and wider it became.

There were walls and walls of books. Some were stacked on the floor, others were made into large pyramids that boggled his over-taxed mind. Books with bindings that he was sure were older than any book he might have seen in libraries before. There were others that were gold. Chris had no idea how he knew that, but he was as sure of that as he was his name.

He moved deeper into the room and saw things that just made him think he was in a dream. There were chairs that moved. Not on wheels that someone might want to roll around, but floating above the floor several inches. When one went by him above his head, he looked up and saw that there were several more there, all of them moving around the room slowly, as if waiting for someone to need them. He looked at Kate, not sure what to say. She laughed at him then, and for some reason he didn't feel any better about what he was seeing, or feeling for that matter.

"I am...we are the keepers of records. In here is every book ever written, every prose that was ever said, and even books on happenings around the world that, while recorded in some history books, these words are truer than any other written. Here are the records of all mankind, and even creatures that walk the earth. Who has been born, those that have died and how they did it, as well their wives or husbands, and any children and their lives as well." He suddenly need to sit down and found himself in one of the chairs. "This room knows you as well as it does me. As I said, we are the keepers now."

"How...how long have you been doing this?" She didn't answer him, but sat in one of the chairs as it suddenly appeared behind her. "You told me that you were over four hundred years old. You're older than that, aren't you?"

"I told you that I was over four hundred years old. That seemed to be a number that you could take. No one wants to know that I have been around forever. That my kind, me and a few others, have been watching over humans, without coming to their aid, for as many years as there have been people here." He nodded, almost afraid to think beyond her being ancient. "I have seen wonders of the world that no one else has. I have witnessed such destruction that I feared no one would survive it. Wonders that I can share with you, but none other. And you must do the same."

"You told Remy that you would help us." She nodded. "You still will. You'll help us conquer this thing."

"You cannot conquer what you don't understand. You should have learned that by now." Shit was running through his head a mile a minute. He looked at her then, and she looked so sad. "Yes, I was there when you were hurt and your wife died. It's the reason that I could see so plainly what you couldn't. Or in that matter, what you didn't want to see. But you knew in your heart that things were not as they were told to you. It was easy to grab your memories and blend them with my own. That date, its written here with all your other history and that of your family. As well as Pella's."

He got up to pace and books moved out of his way as the chair moved back from him and rose to the ceiling. Chris wasn't sure how much more he could take, yet he felt that he needed to know what was going on. Whatever was going on now, he was as much a part of it as she was.

"Do you know if we win this war or not?" He didn't look at her, but watched as a book was opened and words began to appear on the blank page. Moving closer to it, he saw that a babe had been born. Then as suddenly as the name appeared with a date, time, and weight, the same name was put with another date and time. The child had died almost as soon as it had been born. "How does this work?"

"The earth knows everything, and tells me the details by putting them in one of the books that is a part of the whole. Then with our magic, it is written down so that it will be remembered." He asked her who would know that it was here if she didn't allow anyone to enter. "You will know. I know. If you are asked something, a fact that could help you—say the name of the man who might have invented an object you want—you have only to think of him and that information will come to you."

Chris tried not to think of anything, but of course he did. The book in front of him appeared, opened, then the words seemed to jump out at him. The first car, who was there, who had been in the room, and even those people that had been some part of its making in even a small way was on the page in front of him. Dates of their birth as well. People they had married, children born of them. He had only to look at a name and more information would appear. Who the children had married, their children that they'd had, and when they had died. As well as where they were buried and the marker that was there.

Rembrandt was the next person he thought of, and the book disappeared to be replaced by another. As the pages turned, he saw men that had been in his company, the names of his children and wife. He saw the day he'd found them, all burnt to death. He even saw the man who had done it, the one man responsible for so much.

"Benton was his friend. Or so Remy thought." Kate said nothing as he continued to see the murder. The words were so vivid that he could see it as it was written, as detailed as any movie he'd ever seen. "Benton told those men to go to his house to rob him. That Remy had betrayed them all. Then Benton went back and...and he desecrated their bodies."

"Benton is a man that thought he had nothing. He wanted it all, and did not think what he had was enough. The treasures of another were always just out of his reach, even when he took them." Chris turned to Kate and saw that she'd been boxing up things while he'd been getting a lesson in history. "I will gather what I think we will need. You will have to read information on all those that can help us. Nate will...when you have his story, he won't be happy that you do. Be careful how you tread on this man from now on. He is a fuse that is very short. But remember, Chris, you can only tell him what he asks for. Any more will not help anyone, especially him."

Chris didn't think any of them were going to be happy with him knowing everything about them. But he did as she asked and thought of Nate Livingston. He had a feeling that by the time he was finished, he'd have less of an understanding of the man that had been captured by Benton than anyone else.

Chapter 8

Nate hurt. And even when someone came into the room with him, even to check on him, the breeze that accompanied their movements seemed to be spears in his body. Over sensitive didn't even begin to cover how he felt.

He could hear his blood rushing under his skin. Even his hair seemed to be overly loud when he moved his head on his pillow. Sheets sounded like sandpaper, and felt that way too. Nate kept his eyes closed against the bright light, even when it was just the brightness of a candle, he'd been told. Smells made him sick. When Weston came in, it was all he could do not to beg the man to go away. His cologne and deodorant made him think of rotting bodies.

He knew that Weston was doing everything he could. Nate did know that. But it didn't lessen the fact that he wanted him and everyone else to leave him the fuck alone. Or better yet, kill him. He'd been in this room for three days now, and he just wanted to be dead.

He opened one eye when the door was opened and closed.

"Go the fuck away."

Chris said nothing and he started to turn over. He'd been told to be careful of the bed, that his new weight was hard on the metal. Nate moved slowly, but only got his upper body to move before he heard the bed giving under him. He froze, afraid of breaking the bed again and ending up on the floor.

"I can fix that." Chris moved forward, and before he could tell him not to touch him, his finger moved over the bed. "It just needed to be reinforced a little more. You should be all right now to move around. Weston said to tell you he'd be in later to take your blood pressure, by the way."

He did feel...well, not better, but more secure. And when he lay back again safely, he told Chris to get out and leave him to himself. But Chris pulled a chair noisily toward the bed and sat down. Nate put his hands over his ears, trying to stop the noise from tearing his head apart.

"Christ, what is wrong with you? What part of leave me alone do you not get?" Chris said nothing. "Why the fuck can't you people just leave me the fuck alone? I don't bother you; why the fuck do you come in here and bother me?"

"You're an elite shifter. I had to look that up. I mean, I had an idea what it was, but not fully. You're one of the few that can shift into an object regardless of the size, or whether or not it even has a heart beating. Kate, my mate, she's one too." Nate said nothing. It wasn't as if he'd been sharing any information with these people, but no one spoke to him either. No one had asked, and he didn't feel inclined to share. "I also know that before coming here, you were set to kill yourself."

"So? I understand that you're not so thrilled about being here either. Or does getting pussy regular make it all seem okay now?" Nate had expected him to leap at him. At the very least for the other man to tell him to shut the fuck up. But he did neither. Just sat there. "You want more insults? I have them."

"There wasn't anything you could do to save them."

Nate felt his body chill. His blood seemed to stop his heart from beating for several seconds while he waited for Chris to continue.

"Had you been there when they were killed, you would have died too. I know that's what you want now, but it would have done no more to help them. It wasn't your fault that they were killed that day. If you want to know why they did it, then all you need to do is ask me."

"What the hell are you talking about? You have no idea what went on in my life before you got here. So fuck off." But Nate had a feeling that not only did Chris know for sure what had happened that day, he knew his part in it. "I told you to get the hell out, and tell Weston I want to fucking be taken off his IV."

He'd not been able to pull it out. Nate was sure that one or both of the hyped up duo, Remy and Skylar, had made sure that he couldn't, but whatever was in the drugs they were pumping in him, it wasn't doing much for the dull ache where his heart used to be.

"Do you want to know what happened that day, or are you still so set in your grief that you have no desire to hear it? Do you want me to help you? I can. Would you like to know what happened, the truth of it, that day, Nate?" Nate said nothing. He knew what had happened. "No, you don't. You have a version that is in your head, but it's not what really happened. Not the reasons for it either."

"You don't know shit. I'll tell you what happened. Then you can try and fill in what you know. Miriam and her mom were in the kitchen when they entered the house. They killed her mom first, just cut her throat and dropped her to the floor. Blood indicated that Miriam had been hurt there as well. Then Miriam was taken to her bedroom and tied her to the bed after stripping her down. They didn't rape her right away, they were waiting. For what, I have no idea." Nate closed his eyes against the pain of what he'd seen when he'd gotten home. "The children were murdered in their beds. Each of them had had their heart stopped by a single bullet put into it. They just went to each of their rooms and killed them, as if they had no lives to live out and loves to find. I caught them taking them to the living room…that's where I found two of them on the sofa. They wanted me to find them as soon as I came in the door. How fucking sick is that?"

He looked at Chris then, hoping that he'd be like everyone else he'd tried to talk to, sickened to the point of walking away. But he only sat there, his face unreadable, as Nate stared at him. Finally, he told Chris to tell him what he knew.

"The older woman was killed first, but Miriam died soon after. They were dragging her up the stairs to rape her, as you said. She owed them, or their boss…that was why they were there. But she tried to get away and fell down the stairs, breaking her neck in the process. She was dead before they got her to the room." Nate stared at Chris as he continued. "They tied her to the bed after they murdered the children. The men had been told to wipe them out, all of them, and that was just what they did. Each of the children were asleep and never knew what happened to them. Nor did Miriam or her mom."

"No, that's not...what men? How did she owe anyone? I want you to leave here right now." Chris sat there and Nate felt tears roll down his cheeks. "You don't know what happened, do you, Chris?"

"Yes, and you know I do. When you caught them taking the children to the living room, they weren't putting them on display for you, but setting them up so they could take their picture and sent it to their boss. Like I said, they were to clean out the family, erase them from this earth. Would you like to know what happened next?"

"No." But he did, and Chris nodded as if he understood. "They raped her. They...the police said it was brutal."

"It was, but she was gone long before they did it, as I said. They were told they could take more time with Miriam, make her suffer. An accident prevented them from their fun with her while she was living, as I said, but they did make her suffer. The picture they never got to send their boss was to show them that the job had been done. Without it, they wouldn't get paid. Not that they would have. The men were set to be killed too, by Michael James himself. You know who that is, don't you?" Nate said that he knew him...he was a big time boss. "Yes. Miriam had a gambling problem and she was into him for millions. Not only that, but she'd sold out her husband too. She told him that his insurance was huge, and if he was murdered, like he had been, then it would be more. That was who killed him. It wasn't who you thought. What you did was bring them to justice in your own way, and that was the result of it."

"Miriam said...she told me that she was finished. And that now that Conrad was gone, her husband was gone, she knew that she'd have to start saving money. It was...she didn't want to, however. I think she was broke at the end." Chris nodded his head, and that knowing look touched a nerve and his temper flared up. "What the fuck do you know? You weren't there. You didn't see them the way I did."

"No, I didn't, but the earth knew what happened. When you came home you found Sandra, her mother, first. She had been left where she was...it would have been impossible for you not to see her. You entered the house through the basement because you saw the body on the floor when you started to enter through the kitchen, didn't you? You caught them in the act. You found them there and you ended the lives of all those men." Nate looked away, his memories taking hold of him in a tight grip. "The first man you killed, you broke his neck. Dropping him as you went. You were shot twice as the second man came around the corner and saw you. As he was killed, his own gun shattering his chest cavity and the bullet tearing into his heart, you never paused in your pursuit of the children upstairs. Because you didn't want to believe that they'd kill them all, that it had to be a mistake. You also knew that they'd take her there, to the bedroom, to rape, didn't you?"

Nate had known. Miriam had been the target, and he had tried his best not to think of what they might have done to the children. Surely his mind kept telling him, they wouldn't hurt the children for the acts of the mother.

"The man coming down the stairs was next. His body was torn nearly in half when he tried to kill you with his knife. But you let one of your beasts go, and the bear in you attacked even though you were losing blood fast. Then you found the last two in the bedroom." Nate closed his eyes against the memories, but all that did was bring to living color the nightmare he had all the time. "Your anger was fueled by the sight of the children having been murdered like they had."

Nate thought of his friend's wife laying there, her eyes vacant in death. "They were raping her. Not with their bodies but with their guns, shooting her between her legs, telling her that they were coming as they did so." Chris said nothing, and for all he knew he might have left him by then. "I killed the first one when he came at me, shifting in midair even as the wolf took him. But he was no match for my anger, and as he came forward I put out my fist and rammed it down his throat. The second man I...I played with him before the cops came."

"You made him suffer. Made sure that he knew that he'd fucked with the wrong man before he died." Nate nodded. "They called you a hero. The police and the others, they called you that when they found out that you had tried to save a woman and her children that were not your own. They had no idea that you were related to her in any way, did they?"

"Conrad was my half-brother. His wife and children were related to me only because I thought of him as...we thought they'd be safer when he testified if everyone assumed he was an only child. I have no idea why we thought that would work. Miriam had a big mouth and couldn't keep.... I never told a soul that they were my brother's children and wife. That way, if he was killed or hurt because he had ratted out his company, someone would be there to care for them. But I couldn't. He begged me at the end to watch over them for him, knowing that he was going to be killed, to keep them safe, and I failed him." Nate looked at Chris then. "Like I'm going to do here. I'm a failure."

"No you're not, Nate. She failed you. Miriam told them where she was, let the men in the house that day. The man that she owed, he'd been expecting her payment in the form of Conrad's insurance. But she spent it, every penny of it, on her habit." Nate shook his head at Chris. "She did. The man that Conrad had testified against had nothing to do with the death of Conrad's wife or family. I'm sure he might have gotten around to it eventually, but it wasn't him that killed that family. James is...was not one to mess with, but Miriam thought that with her looks and her children, he'd never harm her. She was dead wrong about that."

"No, she'd never do that. She loved her family, and I told her that I'd help her if she needed me." Chris said nothing, but Nate had a moment of doubt then. "She was struggling, yes, but I had put her on a budget, told her that she'd have to start living within her means. But she would never have betrayed...why would someone do that to their own children?"

Again Chris said nothing, but Nate knew. She'd told him, several times, that the insurance had never paid up. Something about premiums not being paid on time. But he had known, even then, that the money had come out of Conrad's check every week. That there was no way that he would have not taken care of it.

"How do you know all this?" Chris didn't answer and Nate looked at him again. "You don't know, do you? You found out a little bit and decided to fill in the rest with bits and pieces that would...I don't know, bring me around to your way of thinking. Well, it won't work. I'm not going to be in this group of idiots that think they can make some sort of difference."

Chris only stood up and moved to the door. Nate wasn't sure, but he thought that he'd just lost something,

something profound. When he found himself in the room alone, he closed his eyes and tried his best not to think about Miriam and the kids. About the many times she'd told him that she needed more. Not just money, but a bigger house, a nicer car. She wanted to go on lavish vacations, sometimes alone. Her mother was no better, telling him that it was his fault that Conrad was dead, that he'd left them penniless.

There had been money, a great deal of it...he knew that. Conrad had a huge life insurance policy, a fat savings account, as well as his inheritance from his own father. When he asked Miriam about it, her answer had amazed and astounded him.

"Mom and I went to the casino." He asked her how much she had lost. "Well, there is enough for us to make the house payment. We were in grief. I had to do something to cheer me up."

She'd lost nearly seven million dollars. All in one day, and for no other reason than she had it. And now, she and her entire family, his family too, were gone.

~~~

Kate walked around the big room and wondered what sort of questions they were going to have for her. There were things she was willing to answer, but there were also things that she could not. When Remy and Skylar came into the room along with the rest of the group, Chris pulled her into his arms for a much needed hug before they sat at the long table.

"What are you?" Kate nodded and told Remy. She liked the big man...he was direct, kind, but he was also a man who got what he wanted, and she liked that as well. "And this keeper of records, what is that exactly?"

"I watch over the things that happen in the world, this one anyway. There are others like me in different realms that do the same. When we need to have information, perhaps on something that occurred there, we can contact them and they can help. Every realm has one." She looked at the people in the room before continuing. "Hector, you've met your keeper. Her name is Adaline. She is the one person on your realm that will never die, but continue long after there is nothing left of your home to keep the records. Then as the world begins to regrow, she will be the one that is there before all others."

"Why?" She asked Skylar what she meant. "Why would anyone need to keep records if there is no one there to make anything happen?"

"But there are other things in the realm that are not human. Trees continue to grow and die, plants reform, adjust to their environment. People might come to the realm, see what is there is and move on. Or stay if they find the planet or realm something that they can work with. And not just plants, but the creatures that live there as well. They go on, function, live, die. It all needs to be kept on record." Hector asked who helped her, or even Adaline. "Some of us take mates; others of us, like me, tried to make a life for myself. Fall in love. Most of the time there is one person for us, and they too will gather and help with the collection of information. I will admit that my previous mate was taken at a time when I was lonely. I should have known that he wasn't for me and avoided that part of my life."

"So not just keeping records of humans, but of all living things." Kate nodded at Vicki. "The earth, she says that no matter what happens to us, the world around us continues. And you keep that knowledge somewhere safe, right?"

"I do. Magic is everywhere, even you know that." Vicki nodded. "There are a few—some with a lot of magic, others with very little—that help me. They don't know it, of course, but their magic sustains the place where the records are stored. And when I need information from another realm, the same magic helps me there as well. Like the monsters that day."

"So you knew those monsters that flew in the sky were from my realm." Kate nodded at Hector. "Could you have told us about them? Warned us that they were coming here?"

"I cannot intercede, nor can I change what is going on. I can only tell what is done." Remy asked her what that meant. "Once they were here, the teratorn, I could help you with them. I could tell you where they came from, how they survived, and who had sent them. But only if you asked me. I cannot give you what you do not want to know. I wouldn't have been able to tell you they were coming. First of all, I wouldn't have known until they were here, and secondly, I cannot predict the future. I can only know what has been done."

"So if we were to ask you, could you tell us if this ends? This war with the other realm?" She shook her head at Remy. "Then I don't understand what you have said. You can help, but you cannot. You can give us information, but we must know to ask it. Is there anything you can tell us that would be helpful?"

"Plenty. But as I said, I don't know what the future brings. I can only tell you what you ask, and only if it's already come to pass." Kate knew that she was frustrating them, but there was no way that she could tell them anything without there being consequences. "Remy, you must ask me."

"I know not what to ask you." Remy stood up and began to pace. "My life before this was so simple. If I needed information, I would simply ask my wife and she knew it."

"Shandell, your lady wife, was a good woman. She did not deserve to die the way that she did." He paused in his motion to look at her. "Yes, I know what happened. I have all the records for every birth and death, and even how it took place. Every blade of grass, every leaf that fell from the trees. Offspring that are born to people, where they lived, and where they're buried."

"I saw that." Everyone turned to Chris. "The first day we were there, at this building, a book was in front of me and it wrote the name down of a child. The date, the time, even how much the child weighed. Then, just as quickly, it wrote the date of death, how she had died, and who was with her when she passed. I read up on some other things as well. Information that I thought might be helpful to someone. Turns out...it doesn't matter how that turned out, but she's right, it's all there."

"Adaline told me once that she knew where all the bodies were buried. That no one could get anything past her." Kate smiled at Hector and the look on his face as what his friend had said to him took on a whole new meaning. "She does know where they are, doesn't she? And the history of...well, all of us."

"Yes. She, like me, is bound to rules that keep everyone safe. Not just us, but those that would come to us for information as well. Telling one of their impending death is not allowed. We cannot tell a person not to get into a car should we know that they are to die in an accident."

Remy paced. She knew that he'd ask her questions soon that she couldn't answer, and she waited for them.

"Then how are we to beat this thing? How are we to save the world?" She told him that the rest of the world was fine. "What do you mean, fine? These creatures are taking over the world. There were, at one time, hundreds of thousands of them. The world is not fine."

"No, Remy, the world really is fine. They—the creatures—are only here, near the mountains and you. When they ventured forth, going to other towns, they weren't able to sustain a life there. Too many people, too much magic against them. But here, this is where they were to be. And once they were able to kill you, as was the plan, then the rest of the world would crumble at their feet. It is here where they needed to start." Chris looked at her before he continued. "I've seen what lies beyond us. Hundreds of miles away from here, this hasn't affected them. A few ventured there, the malefactors, but the humans are living their lives. Going to school. Mowing their lawns. They've only concentrated here, near the mountains and you, Remy."

"I get it." They all turned to Vicki. "I know why that...it's us. We're here because.... Don't you see? We were all brought here so that the malefactors would only come here, for us. Mostly Remy and the stones, but the other men, they came here so that it wouldn't spread."

"What do you mean?" Skylar looked at her and Kate only smiled. "Is she right? They're only here because of us? If that's true then.... I don't know.... What if...what if we were to just give up? Or spread out? Then the concentration would be small enough that we could handle it."

"No, that's not right either, is it?" Kate watched Remy now as he figured it out. "We brought them, the other men, here in order to save the rest of the world. With us here, all of us, the malefactors were working to kill us and left the rest of the world alone. Had we stayed apart, tried to live without the power of all of us, then they would have spread out as well, changing more and more until they were covering every part of this earth and not just a small part of it. And our other halves, they're here because...because we were to save them for us. For our reward, as Hector called them."

"You're both right, I believe. Had you not gathered here, then the world, as we all knew it, would have been gone. There would have been worldwide spreading of the monsters, and nothing would ever have been able to come back from the devastation." Remy sat down and asked her if they could beat this. "Is it your wish to win this war?"

"What a question to ask. Why would I not want to save the world?" He sat there for several minutes, and she could feel his anger. "Yes. I wish this to end. Even if it means my death."

"You are an immortal. All of you are." He nodded, but still looked angry. "Tell me, Remy. Tell me what it is you're thinking."

"Can we save the other world as well?" She told him she had no answer to that. "Why is that? Because it is not your domain? Not your concern? Why can we not have everything the way it once was?"

"Now you're just being cruel. And you know the answer to that as well as I do."

He nodded and looked over at Hector. He knew as well as they did that they could not save the other realm.

As they all seemed to be lost in their thoughts, Kate moved out of the room. There was nothing more that she could do for them at the moment. Remy was a true leader, and once this information was processed, they'd be able to move on. For now, she knew that they each had to work through what they'd figured out.

Chris came up behind her and pulled her into his arms. "Nate is still fighting this. I thought about telling him about his mate, but I couldn't." She didn't say anything. Chris had maybe moved a little beyond the bounds of what they could do, but it wasn't breaking too many rules. "I want to take you back to our room and make love to you until we can't move."

"I love that idea." As they made their way to the part of the building where the bedrooms were, she said nothing. She was, if she was honest with herself—and she seldom was not—tired. Not just of body, but her mind needed a rest too.

Their room. It had nice ring to it. Kate had been living where she could for so long, it was nice to have a place where she belonged. She supposed she could call the library her home, but it really wasn't. It was everyone's home. This place, it felt good. It even smelled like she thought of as a place that she could live forever.

"What happens to us when this is done?" She asked him what he meant, even though it was hard to think with his mouth at her throat. "Do we get to have a place of our own or do we live here?"

"I don't...what is it you want to do?"

He'd pulled her blouse open and was nibbling his way down to her breast. But he was going so slow that she wanted to tell him to either do something or stop and let her do it. But when his mouth covered her suddenly bare breast, it was all she could do to stand upright.

When she was naked, her body warmed by his roaming hands, she watched him as he got down on his knees in front of her and pulled her body to his mouth. As soon as he suckled at her clit, already sensitive by him touching her, she came hard and fast. And she knew that this was just the beginning.

"I love it when you fill my mouth with your cream." Nodding, she wasn't sure she could speak beyond her body readying for him to bring her again. "When this is finished, I want to have children with you. Lots and lots of them."

If she was going to answer, she had no idea what it might have been. Her body bowed back, and her hair felt as if it stood on end as he brought her over the edge and let her fall again. When she felt herself floating, knowing that he was carrying her to the bed, Kate touched him. Anywhere she could feel his naked flesh, she ran her fingers over it, tasting him too.

"Take me." He nodded, his cock at her entrance, then he moved inside of her. It wasn't just fucking, he was making love to her. Wrapping her legs around his hips, locking her ankles, she watched his face, seeing his animals there as they seemed to approve of what they were doing. They loved her. This she knew somehow.

"Come for us." Kate screamed, her body simply obeying his command as if he'd had a gun at her head and ordered her. "Again. Come for us again; we need you to come again."

Her body didn't have time to ready for his command before she was coming again. Adjust to what was happening to all of her. Even as she came a fourth, then a fifth time, she felt his cum fill her, his body claim her as no one had ever done before. When she came again, this time rolling darkness claimed her, and she knew that this man would love her forever. And she would love him as well.

Chapter 9

It was destroyed. Everywhere he looked everything was gone. The lab, the medicine that he needed, every part of it was simply gone. Master looked around for Dolin or Ward. Both of them had been absent for some time now, and he could no longer hear them speaking to him. He could not even get close enough to see if the worker had made him any more of the lovely drug. The fire raged on, taking not just the building, but the ground and the trees surrounding it.

"They're dead, you idiot. Why they kept you around is beyond me. If anything, I believe you've gotten stupider." Mary had been mean to him for hours now, and no matter how many times he'd told her to hush up, she did not heed his commands. "I'm dead too. And in the event that you've not caught on yet, you are going to be stuck here if you do not get back to the other world before they close that down too."

"I wish to stay here and make more creatures for me to rule." She told him there was no one here to change. What was he going to do, shit some people? "You are very rude and I do not care for your tone. I am Master. And I will find them. They hide from me."

"Look at you. You're ugly, falling apart, and you've not a lick of sense. What do you think they're going to do? Hmm? Are you going to stand here, yell for them, and think them to come running here to do as you bid?" She snorted. That was just what he'd thought of doing. "There is no one here for you to change. You've managed to kill an entire race, and are still as dumb as you have always been. When they brought you here all those decades ago, I told Ward you would never do. That you were too stupid to even learn to care for yourself."

"Stop that right now." He could hear her humming, something that she did when she was trying to annoy someone. She'd do it just long enough that you'd speak to her again, and then she'd start again. Master was beginning to hate Mary.

His body was still injured, but it also felt better than it had ever felt. He knew that he was bigger; whatever had done it to him, he was glad for it. Bits and pieces of what had happened in the lab flittered through his mind, but he wasn't able to pinpoint anything. There had been a man in a cage, but he was having trouble remembering if it was him or someone else. Then there was the way his mind kept forgetting things.

Yesterday he'd been standing in an open field, and he could not for the life of him remember what he was there for. As he walked away, sure that he'd done whatever had brought him out there, he remembered that he'd been looking for food. Then this morning, he'd woke to find himself in his cave, but there was no one around. He'd called for Randall for twenty minutes before he realized that the man was no longer alive.

"Rembrandt was here too. He and that woman of his. They took my things." He had no idea if that was right or not. There was something there, pain and blood, but he couldn't think right.

"You're stupid, that's why."

He decided to ignore her for now. Making his way to his portal to see if anyone had come through, he walked past a broken bell. Something about it conjured up images as well, but again, they were too fast for him to catch what it was about. He knew that the ringing of it, the sound, had reverberated in his head, and that it had made him angry. But then lately, everything did.

"I think I shall go back to Rembrandt's world. There I can see about gathering a fold of my own so that we might plan and kill him." That hadn't worked out for him as yet, but he thought that his luck was to change. Mary told him he was a fool. "I'm no such thing. I am Master, master of all that will bow before me."

He would have to find someone to repair him. He was falling apart, and some parts of him were no longer working correctly, like his arm. It was limp now, no longer functioning enough for him to even lift it. Even with the new energy he had, there was something wrong with his body. Looking at himself, he wondered if he'd be better off taking a body to use.

His left arm was useless, but his right seemed stronger for some reason. The left hung down from his body at the shoulder, and would not lift up for any reason unless he did so with his other hand. Well, it wasn't a hand any longer, but a large claw that was difficult to use when he had to dress himself or even scratch his head. Even his claw was missing some of the sharp points at the end. And he could no longer become his other self, just the big monster that made him feel so wonderful. Most of the time anyway.

His body was bigger, yes, but no less sickly. Parts of his scales were missing, some of them broken and burned. He blamed that on the bitch of a woman that had burned him with her white heat. His tail, usually so strong and easy to swing around to keep his rear safe, no longer moved the way it should, mostly just flopping around behind him and getting caught in things. He'd also noticed that he was picking up nasty things with it. Twice now he'd had to stop to pull the dead from the spikes on the tip.

His mind, too, was acting strangely. Along with his recent memory loss, there were times when he could not even remember his own name, his purpose in life, or what he'd done to make himself look like he did. Large gaps were missing from his childhood...his parents and family, or even if he'd had any. Then as quickly as the memories were gone, they'd come back to him several days later with a clarity that he'd never had before.

"You had no parents, I believe. I think you to be hatched from a stone." That hurt, but he said nothing to Mary. Of late she was getting meaner in her comments to him, and when he found her, he was going to talk to her about it. "Yes, you do that. Because you do know that I'll heed every word of it, because *I am dead,* you idiot!" Her shouting at him had him holding his head. When she said nothing more, he made his way to the place where he could go between the two worlds.

The portal was just where he'd left it. It was damaged; some of the magic around it had been tampered with, but he knew that it would take him away. He looked around, wondering if he was forgetting anything, knowing somehow that he'd never return here.

"Not that it matters. I shall rule the other world, and will not even care that this place was here." Mary called him a bastard. "You may call me what you wish, but you will not be at my side. I shall leave you here, with your lovers."

Entering the magic, he closed his eyes. Movements like this, the magic almost seemingly sucking at his body at all the worse places, he wondered if he could find enough men to work for him and if they'd be willing to bring him food. Master realized quite suddenly that he was hungry.

The portal on the earth side of the realm was damaged as well. It took him several seconds to realize that he might have come just in time. As he moved away, his body burning from the magic, he saw the big dragon, dressed as a human, and his mate come out of one of the vehicles that had only just pulled up. Even Remy and that bitch of a mate of his were there. No one, he thought, saw him coming through, for which at the moment he was glad.

He thought about approaching them all. Killing them with his newfound power. But he was weak; lack of food, as well as the magic that had been depleted from coming through, had left him less than up to par, as Ward used to say. Moving back deeper into the wooded area around the group, he watched as they stood around a large building. Then one of them spoke.

"How do we destroy this?" No one seemed to have an answer, and Master wondered why they were doing it in the first place. It wasn't theirs to destroy. They'd not made it. He knew that this was the building that brought him his men, the ones that had tried to help him, but he wasn't really sure how that had happened either. "I'm all for just burning it down, using magic on it, then when we've done that, pissing on it."

"Urinating on it will not improve its unworthiness to us, but I can understand why you think you must do it. Pissing on that will give me a great deal of satisfaction as well." Master wanted to go out and strangle Rembrandt, even tear his head from his body, but he laughed then and Master knew that he would get the man soon. "However, burning it will be the first thing we do. Then when the others arrive, we will have Vicki and Kate work their magic on it as well."

He had names. Master thought about them over and over. Vicki and Kate. He knew Rembrandt and Bitch, but as he repeated them over and over in his head, the reason for doing so was lost. When the building simply burst into flames, all thoughts of names and reason fled his mind as he watched his magic being torn down. *Will these people ever stop trying to destroy me*, Master wondered.

When two women arrived with two more men, Master moved away. He didn't even know why he was there...watching his old friend tear down a building was boring and somewhat stupid. As he made his way to his cave, he thought about things he'd not thought of for years.

"She was no more your friend than I am." Master paused and looked around for Mary when she spoke to him. "Remy's wife was not your friend. She was a woman who was so far out of your realm of friendship that I'm surprised that she didn't make you bathe every time you came to her home. Or take your meals in the barn with the rest of the animals that were stored there."

"Shandell was my friend. Many a time, she would have me over to give her comfort." Master tried to think what her face had looked like, the woman that had loved him above Rembrandt. "We had children together, she and I, and she loved me above all others."

"Lies," Mary screamed at him. "All lies, and you know this. She hated you. Did not want you around her children, and when her husband was away at war, where you should have been, she hid from you, barred you from entering her dwelling so that you could not taint her home. You were even then a monster to her. It is why you killed her, is it not?"

Master felt his anger grow. Even as he entered the cave, he knew that once he released his anger, Mary was going to be.... Master felt a pain in his head as he tried to think of Mary and killing her. At the thoughts of her body, grief so profound that he couldn't breathe around it touched him. He could almost see Ward there, his sadness so great that it took him to his knees. Dolin too. The man had been crying, like a small child who had lost something. They had, in Mary, but his mind wouldn't tell him how.

"What is this trick that you play on me?" She said nothing and he began to pace his new home. "You make me believe your dead. Dolin and Ward, what have you done with them? I demand that you bring them to me. I have a need of their services, and you are an annoyance that I can live without. Where are they?"

"Dead. Like you will be soon if you do not take care of Rembrandt." The words, spoken so softly, nearly had him falling to his knees. He was an immortal, was he not? As were Rembrandt and the people, his enemies that were trying to murder him. "Are you, Benton? Are you like them? If you are, then why are you in constant pain? Why must you take drugs to keep you from hurting?"

"Why indeed." He looked again at his body. "I am injured. What has happened to me? Where did...? Did Rembrandt do this to me?"

"He did. He and his bitch of a mate." Master nodded and sat down at the fire pit in front of him. For a moment he missed what he'd been thinking about. Mary spoke again. "They are going to hurt you to the point where you are nothing more than a broken monster. How will that look when you rule? That someone so meaningless was able to get the better of you for a time?"

"I will rule." She said nothing to him. "I will. Once I have taken care of those men and their mates, I will rule this earth with a hard hand and my magic."

"You will not be able to rule anything if you do not heal. You must have more drugs to heal. Where will you find such drugs?" He had no idea. And what sort of drugs would he use? "Benton, pay attention to me. You must kill Rembrandt."

"Rembrandt is my friend." But that didn't sound true either. Something was there, some memory that just teased at the point where he could see it. "He tried to harm my wife and children."

Again, that wasn't quite right. Children? Master tried to think if he had children and where they were. And a wife? He had never taken a wife as far as he knew, but she was there. Or some memory of her.

"Why can I not remember her?" Mary told him because she was never his. "Yes, she was. We were in love."

No, again, that was wrong. Standing up, forgetting where he was for a moment, he tried to think. Then he saw the drawings on the wall. He moved to them, careful of where he was going for fear of falling again. It hurt him so to try and get back up on his feet.

There were pictures; crudely drawn, but he could make them out for the most part. Of course, whoever had drawn them had put the names of the people depicted in them. Rembrandt was there. A woman simply called bitch and a few others. Looking at the picture of the woman who seemed to have long fingernails at the end of her hands, he saw that she had red on her clothing, and he could only surmise that she'd been hurt. Then he moved along the wall and saw himself.

"I am quite handsome, don't you think?" He had a crown on his head, as well as a long cape that seemed to be flowing behind him. Looking at it, he smiled. Beneath his feet was Rembrandt. "I do believe you're right. Rembrandt and I are not friends. He is trying to kill me. I need to find him and kill him before this gets twisted up in my head again."

Sitting down again at the fire pit, he used a little of his magic to warm himself by starting a fire. The longer he sat there, quietly letting his mind work, he realized a great many things. And most of it was making him angry.

"She never would have me. When I went to her home after Rembrandt had left her alone, she told me to leave her. Leave her? I am much better than Rembrandt will ever be. Yet she turned me away like I was nothing more than the dirt that made her floors." He thought of the children. "Did I tell you that she made them stay away from me? Telling them that they were not to talk with a man such as me? Like I would harm them."

"You were cruel to them. Even the babe when it was wee." He had been. It had been fun to make them cry when no one was around to stop him. "You might have taken better care that she not see you doing it. Things would have gone differently for you had you done only that."

Master warmed his body over the fire, thinking more and more of how he'd been treated by Rembrandt and his family. Also making him wonder why he had not been able to kill Rembrandt sooner. The man was just too nice. His rules, the way he thought all people should do things, were easy to get around. Break one of them, or even all of them, and Rembrandt would forgive you for it. The man would take food from his own table to help someone in need, but never Master.

"Once I went to him and only asked to sleep upon his floor in his home. To warm my body by his fire. Do you know what he said to me? He told me that I would have to earn my keep to do so." Master thought about that time. "Only after a few days he tossed me out on my ear, telling me that no one got ahead in the world by living off the backs of their friends. I had a few words to say to him as well."

"No you didn't. You said nothing. Whined a great deal, telling him that you were too weak to help with the farm. But he did kick you out when you needed him. Rembrandt is a cruel and heartless man." He liked what Mary was saying and asked her for more. "Remember the time that you stole from him? Took his prized horse out of his barn and sold it?"

Master laughed. "He actually told me he was sorry. Sorry that he'd not seen how desperate I was. But then he offered me a job. He said it would help him greatly if I were to help him recoup his money from having to buy his horse back." Master laughed again. "As I have said a great many times, he is a sap."

"You must kill him." Master could see that now. Rembrandt was messing up his plans once again. "You will not rule if he is living. Kill him. All of them must die, but you must start with Rembrandt. The others only follow him."

"I will. I need to make a plan to do so." Getting up, Master went to the mouth of his cave. Looking downward, he could see the compound and the people running about like nothing was wrong. "They will all need to be dead for me to rule."

"Yes. All of them. But Rembrandt must suffer. He killed me." Master nodded, thinking about her death and his love of her. "You remember that, Benton. I was nice to you when no one else was."

Was she? He didn't remember. But she was talking to him now when both Dolin and Ward had left him. His mind tugged at him, feeling like it was trying to tell him something else, but he moved back into his cave. It was time to settle this. Past time. He should have killed Rembrandt when he was on the battle field with him.

~~~

"Try a bear." Chris let the animal take him as he held onto Kate. They were having fun, something that they all needed after the previous day. "Damn, but that's a fine bear."

Today was for not working, if they didn't have to be, but for experimenting on things. Like their ability to change into different animals and merge. So far it had worked well. There had only been one that they could not take on together, and that was a dragon. Leo thought it was perhaps because they had one of those, and there was no need for a second one. Remy said it sounded like a solid reason to him as well. There had been a scare yesterday that had had them needing this day more than ever.

Remy had gone into the grocery that they had set up several weeks ago and had been injured. He'd only gone there to check on supplies, something that was as mundane as walking, he told them. But he'd been ambushed. Not hurt badly, but enough that Skylar had felt it too. When she'd taken to the skies without a word, they all had followed. He supposed now it was a good thing that they had.

Remy had been unconscious on the floor, several malefactors standing over him and beating him with bats. Skylar was fighting with an adherent, something that none of them had encountered for some time, when and Kate had entered. As the adherent had tried his best to take off Skylar's head, Kate and the rest of them had tried to help. It had been a trap.

Several more adherents had come out of the woodwork then, nine total, and each of them bent on taking someone's head off, the only way that they could be killed, apparently. Their blades had been razor sharp and covered in what they discovered later to be the blood of the dead. They had no idea if it worked on them the same way as it had on Hector and his family, but they had worked hard in not letting it touch them.

Chris had been swinging his blade at his man when he stopped suddenly and smiled at Chris. He'd been so caught off guard that it had taken him a full minute to realize that he should have killed the man when he had the chance. Instead, he waited for him to tell him what was so funny.

"You will all be dead soon. And when you are, we will rule this world like we should have from the beginning." Chris said nothing. "We will rape your women, burn your homes, and run off all of your livestock."

"My livestock?" The man nodded, his bluish skin making him look sickly against the lighting of the store. "And I'm pretty sure that if you try to rape my mate, she will pull your dick out and feed it to you. Besides, I'm pretty sure that you can't have sex. It's because of your nasty disposition."

"I will father the next king." Chris laughed. "You will see. We will rule this world and you will be our servants."

"How the hell does that work? I mean, if you kill me, I can't very well be your servant, now can I? I don't think you've really thought this through, have you? Perhaps you can go home, make a plan, and we'll take up where we left off. Sound good to you?"

The man growled low. Chris flipped his sword at him and nearly cut him when he was shoved from behind.

Benton had come in the front of the building. Not the door, but the entire front of the building. Chris had known that he was bigger, but now he looked...he wasn't sure how to describe the man's size. It was fucking big. His claws on his one hand had looked sharp and dirty as he swiped at Chris, narrowly missing his neck.

The next several minutes had been tense. None of them could seem to get close enough to him to do more than piss him off, and when Vicki had raised her hands up to hit him with her magic, she'd been knocked back and the adherents had fallen atop her, making it impossible for her to do much more than keep them from taking off her head.

Come to me. He looked at Kate when she spoke and she waved him to her. *Come on. We need to be bigger.*

As Chris threw himself in her direction, Benton hit him again. His large claws had entered his belly and torn through him as they exited his other side. When he was lifted up, nearly to the man's mouth, and was probably going to have his head bitten off, Chris was dropped as Kate and Vicki came together and used their magic.

Benton screamed at the pain, and Chris knew it was painful because there was a hole burning in Benton's belly. Chris tumbled across the floor, his body healing almost immediately. And when he touched his hand to Kate, just a simple brush of his fingertips to her skin, the surge of energy nearly took him to his knees. Standing up, feeling invincible, he began chasing after Benton until he took to the skies.

"Do you suppose that when we're all one, all twelve of us here, we'll be a force so mega that the world will never be the same?" Chris looked at Remy when he spoke, his voice soft and tight. It brought him from his memories of the battle, and it took him several seconds to try and focus on what he was talking about. "I should like to think that it wouldn't have happened, but after today, I'm not so sure. The power of us together...it was more than I had thought we'd have."

The power of the two women together had blown out the back of the building, and Benton with it. And when they broke apart, their bodies had been drained so badly that they'd had to be carried to the car. Had they known or even thought of it, they said, they would have turned their power on Benton and been done with it.

"They took out four buildings with their magic as it was. Can you imagine what it might have done to Benton had they hit him with it?" Remy nodded, still watching as Kate shifted from animal to animal to delight the children that had come to watch them working. "Power like that...if the other women can add to it, it would be enough to take out Benton, don't you think?"

"I should think so, but I'm not sure about much of what we do." Which was true. Ruben had put together a book on the computer and had printed them each a copy. It was thick with information about each of them. And there were even spaces for the members and their mates yet to come. Rick's mate, as well as Nate's, if he would have her. "When we are finished, if we should be able to do this, do you think to have a normal life?"

"Define normal for me and I can answer that." Remy just nodded at his attempt at a joke. "Yes. I'd like to think we can. Kate and I want to have children. And I know that you and Skylar have talked about it."

"Aye, we have. But will they be like us? Will they be born as we are, tatted and with power so great that they will be hunted? Will we be hunted? The other day when you told me about the rest of the world going on as if nothing were amiss...those people, do you think they'll think us the monsters? Will we be required to live alone? Be shunned by those that we have given our all to save?" Chris said nothing as Remy continued. "I should like to know that we will be respected. Thought of as helpers of this world and not the bad fellow."

"You could never be the bad guy, Remy." Remy thanked him for the correction. "You're a wonderful man, and if they can't see that, maybe we would be better off staying on our own."

They were both quiet for several minutes. Chris was thinking about the puppies and how they had been sent to them. He wondered not for the first time since the little guys had arrived if Bob had known all along that the children as well as the adults would get so much enjoyment out of them. And it was just what they had all needed.

"What if, like the house, you can adjust things to suit what you need?" Remy asked him what he meant. "I'm not sure, but what if you can make it so people only see what you want them to? No tats if you didn't think they'd like that. No magic that would scare the shit out of the most calm man or woman. What if, like the building that had been set up here, you were just what people wanted you to be for them?"

"I think that, even though a good thing, would be sad. Do you not? Who would want to be someone different for other people?" Chris told him that people did it every day. "I am sure they have been, but it is not something I would wish to be. I should like to be the man that I am. Just like the man that I am to everyone."

"I wasn't talking about your personality. I mean your appearance. What if—and this is a huge fucking if—what if a person that had no magic only saw Rembrandt, and not Rembrandt, warrior of old, who daily was covered in blood from the actual monsters that went bump in the night?"

"I would bathe it off, but I think I see where you are going with this." They were silent for several more minutes. "How would we test this? This guess of yours."

"I haven't a clue. We could maybe go to one of the towns where there are just regular people, but I'd be afraid of being arrested or something." Remy nodded. "I mean, we'd have to be careful with it. Send out someone that we trust. Someone that can blend in.

"Perhaps we should simply wait. If we were to test this and the malefactors followed, we would be endangering those people as well." Chris hadn't thought of that and nodded. "But when we do, I should like to have you go with me. That way, when I need someone to rescue me again, I shall only need to call upon your large cat and have them eaten alive."

Remy moved away from him after saying that, and Chris was left to wonder things. Had he been joking? Did he really want him to eat a human who didn't care for the way he was made up? Chris was still sitting there when a dark shadow fell over him, and he reached for his sword even as the children ran for the shelter of the house.

Chapter 10

Kate watched the large monster fly back and forth. They weren't sure if he was looking for a place to land on them or he was simply waiting for them to make the first move. Whatever it was, they were all standing there watching him, waiting for something to happen.

"Perhaps he is wishing to see if he could shit on us." Kate turned to Rick and wondered just for a moment if he was right. "I mean, look how high he is. Even if he were to swoop down on us from that height, we could easily run for cover. And if nothing else, we could walk to the house and be done with him."

"But he can't cross over the line, right?" Rick told her that was his understanding as well. "Then why just fly overhead? I know that it's exhausting flying, and he's got to still be weak from when we saw him the last time."

"I don't know."

Neither did she, but she could find out. But Kate was afraid to leave them to do so. Instead, she made her way to Vicki and asked her to find out what the earth had to say.

"He was holed up in a cave until an hour ago. The same one that he was in before. Jake and Jarvis have taken to the woods to go and find out what happened to the camera that they had set up there. They're upset that they didn't know that he'd been living there for a few days." Kate said nothing. She knew that Benton had returned and that he was insane, but little else. Kate had told them this the first time she figured it out, but she had no real insight on what he was doing. "This magic that you have, can you tell me if you can see your future, or just everyone else's?"

"I can't ever see the future. Not even before I met all of you." She asked her if she could see enough in the earth to figure things out about her and Davis. Kate started to tell her that she'd gone over this before, but knew that Vicki was asking for reassurances rather than her to tell her what she could not. "The only thing I can see is about others around us, things that they have done already. Catherine and Jarvis will have a child of their own soon...she's breeding now. Weston has cut his hand again, but not as seriously. Catherine has stitched him up."

These were things that were going on, normal things that had nothing to show her about what the future might hold for any of them. Most of the time it was up to the person to change their outcome. She knew the present and the past, very little about the now, and even less about the future.

As they watched, Benton flew lower, his wings touching the ground around the encampment. But he never breeched the area that was covered in magic. Kate wondered aloud who had put up the barrier in the first place.

"Remy and Skylar. They thought for a long while that Hector had done it. But he told them that he didn't have that kind of magic to work with. The same with the building. When a room is adjusted that we're in we do that to help ourselves. But only in our own rooms or a room that we have claimed sort of for our own. The rest of the house, like the lands here, are the magic of those two." Kate wondered about that too, how hers and Chris's room had seemed larger to her. "So you think that this will all disappear when the malefactors do? Do you think that we'll just be normal? Whatever that is."

"I have wondered, as I'm sure a lot of us have, what happens to this place when there are no more wars to fight." Vicki asked her if she thought that was possible, that the world would never be at war again. "I guess not. But do you think that, say, we all built our homes here, that the magic would protect us?"

"I need to believe that it will. And by protecting us, I'm assuming you mean from humans and what they do when they find something that they don't understand." Kate nodded. "Yes. I believe that we will be safe here, if for no other reason than we will have each other."

Benton came down from his lofty height and circled the compound twice. As he landed then, his big mutilated body sitting just on the barrier of their land, no one moved, not even to draw their weapons. Kate really didn't see him as a threat right now, nor apparently did the others. She watched as he huffed at them, his hot breath not even scorching the ground on their side of the magic.

"Where is he?" Kate was pretty sure he was asking for Remy, but no one answered him. "Rembrandt. Show yourself so that I might kill you."

"You think you might, but I do not believe that you will be able to." Remy stood there, his arms crossed over his chest, and laughed at him. "You are no match for me,

Benton. You never were. What is it you hope to accomplish by coming here, showing yourself for what you are to us? Scare us? Not likely. Harm us? You know as well as I that it is not possible. What is it you want?"

"Come here. I wish to have you on equal grounds to me." Again, Remy laughed but didn't move. "You are not playing fairly; you know this, do you not? Come here, let us fight like men, and I will let your mate live for a bit longer."

"I would be more afraid of her than of me, Benton." Benton screamed at him to stop calling him that, his name was Master. "Not to me it is not. You rule neither here nor anywhere so long as I breathe. You are nothing more to me than an annoying fly that bothers the ass end of a horse."

"You insult me? Me? I am.... If you were to do as I say, then I will be ruler, a master of all. Come now, you owe me that much. I wish you dead, Remy. I have a great army coming for you and your men. We have figured out a way to—"

"You lie." Kate moved forward and stared at Benton from her side of the yard. "You're a liar. You don't have shit and you know it. You should know that I can...I can see the future, Benton."

"No one can see the future. You are the one that lies. And who are you to dare tell me that I do not tell the truth? Be gone, before I put you at the top of my list of those that have angered me." Kate laughed at him and she could see that it pissed him off. "You are nothing but a mere woman who will be raped by my horde of men."

"Horde? I don't think so. And besides, we all know that your less than manly parts don't even work. You couldn't get a hard-on even if there were hundreds of naked women clamoring all over your nasty body trying to suck you off." She made a point of looking in that general area, and then looked back up at the monster's face. "You have nothing that interests me. Not to mention, you really do look like yesterday's garbage. What did you do to yourself?"

"I have done nothing. This is what these men have done to me." He lifted his wings up, and she could see that it was hard for him to even hold himself up in the air. "I am going to be repaired soon. I have men working for me now, and they will —"

"Lies again." She looked at Remy, then back at Benton. "Did you hear me when I told you that I can see the future, Benton? I can. And the one that I see has you lying dead in a pool of your own blood, broken and burned. And not by this man. But by all of us. We will win this war against you."

"Now who is lying?" He threw back his head and laughed. "I am now making an army to come and take you all. You'll see. I'll defeat you, then this world will be all mine."

Closing her eyes, she reached into the books. Finding Benton's name, it took her only a few seconds to see what he'd been doing. Or in this case, what he'd been trying to do. When she felt arms wrap around her from behind, she knew it was Chris and that he was adding his strength and support to her.

"You found some agates, didn't you? Found them and broke them into several pieces to spread them out among the few men that you were able to lure to you. But it didn't work. You only managed to murder the people you tried to change. Then when that didn't work, you began tearing off bits and pieces of yourself, thinking that with your newfound power you could create a group of adherents that would not just kill, but be servants to you for all time." She watched his face, or what was left of it, as he stared at her. "The men that attacked us the other day, they were all that was left of the adherents from the other world. There is no army coming for us. There are but a handful of malefactors left. And you are dying."

He roared at her, his great tattered wings spreading out to an impressive size. As Benton continued to scream at her that she lied, tell her that she was nothing to him, Chris asked her if what she was saying was true.

He did try to use the agates as I have said. And those men died. But the rest I've made up. Chris laughed. *Have you noticed that the angrier he gets, the more his color fades out? Like those malefactors that are newly changed as opposed to the ones that have managed to survive.*

He is really dying. She nodded at him and held his body closer to hers as they watched the monster take to the sky, his anger having no outlet on them. *We need to talk to Remy and the others about this. If he really is fading when he gets angry, then we need to step up or gang up on him.*

I would much rather you take me back to our room and continue making love to me like you started this morning. He kissed her neck and then bit down hard. *You're going to make me come if you keep that up. And what will the others say?*

They were suddenly in their room and she was naked. Chris was, however, fully clothed. When she moved to him, he stopped her with a lift of his hand as he sat down in the chair that she was sure wasn't there before.

"Touch yourself for me." Kate asked him what he meant. "I want to see you pleasure yourself. I've given this a great deal of thought, and I really want to see you coming. Your body tensing up. Then when you do, I'm going to eat you. Not nicely either."

"Your cat is going to eat me, isn't he?" He nodded and leaned back in the chair more, his feet stretched out in front of him. She wanted to have him naked, his body laying out before her like a feast that was only hers to sample. "Let me see your cock. I want to imagine it while I play."

"All right. But I'm not going to touch you until I'm ready." He was naked then. His body not just lean, but hard, rock hard, and his cock was thick and stiff. "I'm going to shift when you come, eat your pussy until my cat is happy, then I'm going to fuck you until you're hoarse from screaming."

Nodding, Kate ran her fingers over her nipples and felt them harden, almost to the point of pain. She was going to make him suffer in ways that she thought she was going to enjoy more than him.

~~~

Brave words, he realized seconds after telling Kate he wasn't going to touch her. He wanted to in the worse kind of way. His cock hurt, his body ached to come inside of her. Hell, he would have just liked to have come. Chris watched her as her fingers entered her pussy.

"Christ. That's it baby, play for me." Her fingers were wet, juices slid down her thighs. He wanted to chase it with his tongue. Lap the trail it was leaving with his tongue before burying his mouth over her pussy and feasting. "Spread your legs."

Chris couldn't believe he'd begged her to do that. He was suffering now. And when she did as he said, opening her legs by putting one foot on the bed and the other on the floor, he nearly leapt to her. Instead, he wrapped his hand around his cock and slowly masturbated as she made him hurt. It was by far the most painful fun he thought he'd ever had.

Her hands and fingers were everywhere. His cat hummed along his body, making him know that he wanted his mate as well. When Kate paused and looked at him, he wondered if she could feel his cat as well, and nearly asked her when she spoke.

"My body feels like it's on fire. I want to come, really hard, too, and all I want to do is make this pleasurable for you." He told her he was enjoying her. Understatement, but it was almost more than he could speak. "Good, because...oh Christ, I'm going to come."

Her body stiffened as if it were on the edge of a pinnacle that only she could see. And when she bowed back, her fingers dancing in her pussy while her other hand held onto her breast, Chris saw her climax consume her.

Her hair flew up around her head. Her magic burst from her as well, creating a light halo around her that he was sure was holding her together. Her scream of release sent shivers down his spine, drew his cat forth, and he took him. As soon as he leapt forward, tossing Kate to the bed, he buried his mouth over her pussy and drank greedily from her as she came four more times.

"Please. You have to stop." He didn't. His cat hadn't had his fill, and Chris wanted him to be as satisfied with her as she was with him. When his fur was pulled hard up from her, his cat snarled at her and Kate smiled. "You're killing me. Please, finish me so that I can die a happy woman."

His cat snarled at her then licked her thigh. He knew seconds before he bit her that the cat was going to mark his mate. And as soon as he sank his teeth into her, tearing into her tender flesh, Chris told Kate he was sorry. Sorrier than he'd ever been before. As soon as he lifted his head from her body, his cat let him go and he was a man again.

Chris crawled up her body as himself. His cock was burning now. The need to empty, fill her, was making him slightly on edge. Sliding into her, feeling her tighten around him as he did so, Chris took Kate's mouth as he fucked her.

"I'm sorry, but I need you. Come for me again, baby." She nodded, her body responding once again to his command. The strangle hold she had on his cock, the way she seemed to milk him, was nothing compared to the way that she held him to her, the bite of her nails digging deep into his muscles as he felt his balls curl into his body just before he released inside of her.

The climax took his breath away in its beauty. It was like he was given a second sight into love and romance. Her body and his, so closely tied together that it was as if they were one. He could see everything about her...the way her blood rushed through her veins, her heart pounded in her chest. And finally the way her lungs filled to release the scream that echoed around his head. And when she came again, bringing him over the edge with her, Chris let the darkness take him, much like a good sleep.

When he woke he was alone in the bed. Sitting up, he could see Kate sitting in the window seat. She had a pillow or two behind her and a blanket wrapped around her body. When he said her name, instead of turning and talking to him, she spoke while looking out the window.

"When I was created long ago, the woman told me that someday I'd meet a man that would change my life. That he would, in one night, create things within us that no one had ever dreamed possible for me. And that through it all, I would have doubts about not him but myself, and the fact that he loved me." She turned to him then. "I do. Have doubts about myself. I'm afraid that, once you get to know me, you'll want to go away and leave me."

"I won't. I can't. I need you. Not just as my mate, but everything about you. I love you very much." He started to continue telling her that when she shook her head, but he decided on another path. "When I was growing up, my parents, along with about all my friends' parents, were divorced. It seemed the norm rather than the unusual. Even as mates, my parents were not suited to each other. My mom was just as vicious as him, and they let it spill over into our lives too much for us to feel good about life in general. Then this family moved in down the street. There were three kids, all of them older than any of the kids that I hung out with on our block. Jade was the girl and the boys were Stanley and Markus."

"The Huston's." He nodded, forgetting that she would know this about him. "Their parents were an oddity. Nice and sweet, but it was odd that they were still married for that time frame. People would divorce and marry like they changed their clothing, making no effort to try and work things out. Disposable was the way I thought of it back then."

"Yes. And as the months went on and me and my buddies grew braver, we started to see that while we thought them odd because they were all still one big happy family, they really weren't. Odd, I mean. Mrs. Huston didn't work outside the home—another first—but she stayed at home and baked cookies and made dinner for them all every night. Mr. Huston was a lawyer, a very nice man who wore horn-rimmed glasses and a tie, even on the weekends." Chris leaned back on the headboard and thought of them. "Jade babysat when my mom needed someone to watch us. Even for a couple of hours if Mom was working late, Jade would come over, bring her homework, and hang out with me and my younger brother. She didn't treat us like we were messing up her plans for the night, but showed us things of wonder, like popcorn that had its own pan. How to make real hot cocoa and not mixed with water. Silly things that my parents never showed us because they were too busy hating each other. Jade's mom would send us cookies and pies. Sometimes when there were leftovers at her house, we'd have meatloaf and ham slices so thick that a bite was too big for your mouth."

He knew after a few years that his mom was struggling terribly. There were times when he knew she wasn't eating dinner or any other meal when there wasn't enough to go around for the three of them. His dad had been required to send them money each month, to help with the bills, school supplies, and even winter coats. Chris remembered his mom arguing with his dad on the phone, and her crying at night when the power would be shut off because her checks would only go so far with two growing boys.

"That first Christmas the Huston's were on the block, we got an envelope of cash in our mailbox. I don't remember how much it was. I'm sure it was a lot for us. My mom cried then too, telling us that someone was watching over us." He'd known even then that it was the Huston's…that they had seen how they were living and what they were going through. They'd had a feast that Christmas, their first in all his life that he could remember. There was turkey and a ham, potatoes and gravy. They'd had fresh bread that they hadn't had to pull the mold off of. And butter. The creamy kind, not the kind that seemed to be more water than cream. He remembered being at home with his brother and mother on New Year's Day too.

"Then, a week after Christmas, Mr. Huston came to our house. It wasn't quite dark out yet, but it was slick with snow. He had on this coat that I thought looked warm enough to keep us all from freezing." Chris thought it strange the way memories of things seemed so silly after a time, yet seemed so right when you first thought of them. "Mr. Huston came into our house that day and asked to speak to us. He had a thick envelope in his hand and a police officer with him. When we were all seated in the living room, the television muted, Mr. Huston started speaking. My father was dead, he told us."

"He'd been in a boating accident. He'd been there on his own boat with a woman and a crew." He nodded and asked Kate to come and sit with him. When she was beside him, her body wrapped around his, he kissed the top of her head. "He'd been on a boat that he owned with a woman that was carrying his child. The two of them and all of the crew were killed when the boat stalled and your father tried to start it on his own. He had no idea what he was doing, but wanted to impress the woman he was going to marry soon."

"Yes. Mr. Huston told us that because there was an insurance policy and back child support involved, Mom was going to be able to claim his estate for us. And that he would represent her if it went to trial. He told us that while the woman was not my father's wife, his family thought that they should be entitled to his millions. Millions, he told us. My father had had millions, and it was going to be all ours, he said." He often wondered if there had ever been a thought in his dad's head about him or his little brother. "He said that if there was any cash in the house, it also belonged to us. Mom sat there for the longest time after they left, just staring at the money that had been pulled from yet another envelope that Mr. Huston had brought with him."

His mom had set him and his brother down the next morning and told them what she wanted to do. Chris thought even now that his mom was the bravest woman he'd ever met. That was until he met Skylar and the rest of the women in this house. But she talked to them that day like she valued them and their opinion as to what she thought they should do with the money.

"She said that she loved us both more than anyone would ever be able to explain to us. That one day, when we were older, a woman would come along and we'd have two choices to make. One was that we would flitter it all away on broken promises and half-baked ideas. Or we could love like there was never going to be another tomorrow, and tell this woman that we loved her every single day of the rest of our lives together. Then she looked at the money." Kate looked up at him then. He wanted to tell her again that he loved her, but wanted her to know, in his own words, what his mother had done for them. "She told us that the money was all she was going to take from our dad. That he'd made promises to someone else, and since they weren't as used to him and his lies and broken promises as we were, they should have the rest. Mom said that she loved Dad, despite what he'd done to us…loved him with all of her heart, but he'd never believed her. She said that we needed to make our own way in this world, that we'd never appreciate it as much if we didn't work for it. And having that money, even the little that we were going to take, was going to go to making our lives better, not used for things that mattered little in the long run."

Chris lifted her chin up so that her eyes were level with his. After kissing her gently on the mouth, taking as much of her love as he was giving her, he pulled her back to his chest and put her head over his heart.

"My heart only beats for you. My body only lives for you." He held her tighter. "When my mother told me that I should tell my other half that I loved them without fear, I didn't know what she meant…until now." Kate looked at him. He took her hand in his and put it over his beating heart. "You hold within your hand my heart. I give it to you freely. I love you with all that I am and will ever be. I will worship you forever, keep you as safe as humanly or shifter possible. I love you, Kate, and will until my heart no longer beats."

Chris held her long into the night. He wasn't sure if she believed him, or if she ever would, but he was going to make it his mission to tell her every day for the rest of their considerable lives together. And when the alarm sounded deep within the house, he held her tighter, knowing that they were next in line after this call. His memories, now risen from the depths of his heart, settled over him like a warm worn blanket.

His brother had died when he was eleven and Chris thirteen. A fall from a swing had broken his neck when he'd been playing in the school yard one afternoon. The teacher, a woman of considerable size, had held his hand the entire time that the ambulance had taken to get there. Chris, also there, never left his brother's side, even when the medic had told him to move back. This was his brother, and he was supposed to watch over him. He told him that he was there for him and would not leave him. Brent had died three days later without ever opening his eyes.

Chris knew that his mom had taken it hard. Much harder than he'd ever thought. He missed his brother as well, still thought of him every day, and about things that he wished they would have been able to do together. But his mom, with all the losses that she'd endured, had not been able to survive yet another blow to her life.

Two months after Brent was buried, Chris had come home from the same school to find Mr. Huston in his yard again, this time with another police officer. His face was telling. Even before he spoke, Chris knew that his life was never going to be the same, that yet another tragedy had entered his heart. Mr. Huston told him what he and his mom had talked about a few weeks back.

"You're to come and stay with us until you think you can move out on your own. I welcome you there, all of us do, into our home, as you are already a part of our hearts." Chris asked what had happened to his mother, and said that he was a teenager now and deserved to know. "You do, and I'm sorry about this son. But she's gone. Her heart broke. And no matter how hard she tried to get it to work again, it just couldn't take it anymore."

"Did she kill herself?" Mr. Huston had told him no, that she'd fallen asleep and had simply not woken up. "But she's gone now. She won't have to worry over me again."

"She will forever worry about you, Chris, even in death. That is our job as parents…to worry forever for our children. Just because the heart stops beating for a time here on this plain does not mean that the love stops being there."

Chris had nodded and gone into the house to gather what he would need for a couple of days. Mr. Huston told him that they'd take care of the rest later.

Chris fell asleep then, when the memories of that time seemed to fade out. He dreamt of children running up and down a street, of tatted parents standing on the porches watching over them. And when he felt his body warm more, he knew that Kate had pulled him into her arms and that he was safe there. And would be forever. Chris was in love, and knew that she loved him as well.

Chapter 11

Master was surprised when the creature turned and looked at him. Before when he'd tried to create one with just a small part of the stone, the thing had died horribly. Not that he cared, but the thing had flopped around the building floor so much and made such a mess that he'd had to work for nearly two hours to get someone to come in and clean it up.

Tom, the name on the shirt had said before Master had worked on him. It took him several seconds to realize that the man was clueless as to what had happened. Just as the others had been when he changed them.

"You will go out and find me other men. Ones like you, brave and strong." Tom continued to stare at him. "I give you that order as your new master. You will obey me over all others, do you understand me?"

Nodding, Tom turned and left the building. If he did what he wanted, Master was going to be so happy he might make the man his first in charge. But he turned to the meager amount of stones he had left.

He'd had more than this, so many that he'd had to put them all over the cave to keep them safe. And after finding several of the first creatures—malefactors, Rembrandt called them—and trying to change them, he'd only had little success. Then there had been the trap he'd set for Rembrandt's people.

Master was sure that he'd had them right where he needed them to be. Five adherents were there, as well as the few malefactors that he'd been able to summon to him. But Rembrandt's people had come in force, come to his trap armed and ready to do battle, thus killing his creatures.

"And they took what did not belong to them." His stones had disappeared, along with the men he had sent to kill them. "Nor did they die as they should have."

No one was doing as he had commanded. The malefactors that he'd turned had died almost immediately when he'd told them not to. Mary would never shut up. Ward and Dolin had abandoned him, even though he had told them over and over that he was going to need their help. His ability to go to the other realm was gone now; he had no idea how to go back there, and he knew that had to do with Rembrandt and the people in the compound. Even though he'd told them several times to die, they continued to try their best to thwart him in all his work to become the ruler of this realm. It was not fair how they were not doing as he wanted them to.

"Had I not been talking to you, you would not have figured out how to make more men to carry out our plans." He had to agree with Mary on that one. "I'm always correct, Benton. You should know this by now."

"I do. I do." He moved to the window of the building he was using. There were several people roaming around. He supposed that he could go and kill them, but he wanted to be sure to have a large army when the time came. And killing the people now would lessen his chances of getting that done. "They think that they are without a leader. I should go and show them that I am here for them to bow before."

"You'd only make them afraid of you. You need to have Rembrandt dead. That is the only way you can be fully healed." Master paused in his thinking to listen to Mary. "Yes, you know that as well as I. Once he is dead and the magic that he has stolen from you is yours again, you will heal. You know that it should have been yours. Hector didn't give it to you as he should have. This is his fault as well. When I was working with Dolin and Ward, I told them not to let Hector pick. We knew then that you were going to be the one to make us very rich. But would they listen? No, they did not."

"I should have been the one that they gave such riches to, as you said. Now I have to kill Rembrandt so that I can finally have what was mine from the first." Mary told him that they were being paid to try and kill him. "By who? Who is trying to kill me? I don't need more people coming for me. I have work to do."

"Rembrandt and the others. They're being paid even now. The realm pays them all with riches from my realm. And from what Ward told me, it is quite a sum too. All of them, they get money weekly, I was told." He asked her if she knew how to stop it. "No. The realm is closed to us. I have told you this before, Benton. We cannot go there and stop anything."

Master felt his temper rise up, and could also feel the darkness consuming him. He knew, just as he faded from his mind, that when he woke he was going to have killed the people below. They would not know that their master had done it to them.

When he woke he was in his cave. The walls were wet, he could see that, and when he blew on the now cold fireplace, he had a roaring fire within minutes. When it was bright enough to look around the room, he stared at the destruction.

The walls were covered in...he thought it blood, but wasn't sure whose it might have been until he stood up. The body, or bodies, he found out after a search—not two, but five arms—lying about were more than likely the humans' from below his building. He wanted to mourn their deaths, but not because he was sorry for what he'd done. More because they would not have the honor of serving him.

As he made his way out into the night, he looked around for more of the body parts. He found a vehicle, a large one, much like the one that Rembrandt and his crew used, and was excited for several minutes. Then he realized that it had no one in it that he knew. Whoever they were and why they were up here on his mountain was of no matter now. They were dead and he was not.

Taking to the skies, Master looked at the world below him. "Stupid people should learn to better care for me. It has been too long since I started this until now." His head hurt and when he landed, he felt all over himself, looking for the source of the pain. "Must have hit myself."

"You need more drugs." He was both happy and pissed to finally be hearing from Dolin. "You know that it's the kind that must be taken daily or you will die. Find someone to make it for you."

"No one will work with me." Dolin told him that he was master and that he could make them. "But to find the right people to work for me is what I do not know how to do."

"They have a chemist in that building. I would bet that it is one of the ones that worked for me. You should go there now and demand that they come back to you. It isn't fair that Rembrandt have all the good workers on his side." Master thought that was true. "He's been stealing from us all this time, and Hector has let him. He needs to die as well. Do not forget that when you go there to kill Rembrandt. Think of all the things that Hector has done to us as well."

"I will kill them all." Dolin told him that was an excellent idea. "Of course it is. It is mine, is it not?"

"You are very smart, Benton. Why did we not see that before?" Master smiled and wondered the same thing. "You should go and see the building. Hopefully that fool Tom has brought you more creatures."

"I was just thinking that as well. And while I'm there, I should like to set me up a room of my own. Perhaps in the sub levels; that way I can hear when I am being set upon."

He moved through the town, or what was left of it, and paused in front of a store that he'd not seen before. Or hadn't really given much thought to. As he moved into it, tearing out the front of the place to make it bigger to accommodate his new size, he noticed that the place had been ransacked. Several times, he thought.

In the back was a chemist's area. The shelves had been broken down, bottles were all over the place. He picked up several of them and tossed them away. Master could not read, and thought it rude of the person to have put nothing more than words on the bottles instead of something easier for him to figure it out.

There was a large vault there as well, and it looked like someone had tried to blow it open with blasting powders. Scorch marks ran up the walls and had burned a good deal of the roof away as well. Master only had to put his hands on the door and rip it away. Inside he found more of the same...more bottles; bigger, yes, but bottles with words on them. No pictures, which would have gone a long way in helping him with knowing what he had.

"You should eat them." He looked around for a person that Dolin thought he should eat. "Not a person, but the drugs. Take them. As many as you can fit in your mouth. It's not like it will kill you. Unless there is a sword in the bottles that will remove your head."

The laughter made his skin crawl. Master was sure that it sounded just like Rembrandt's, and even looked over his shoulder to see if he was there. But he was alone in the building, save for the few dead that were there rotting in the corners.

"What if they were to make me sick?" Dolin said that he'd been sick before. "Then what if they do not work and I am still the same?"

"Then you have nothing to concern yourself with. This is the thing you've been looking for, isn't it?" It was. But there were so many. "Take them all."

Master started opening the bottles and decided that there were just too many, so he began simply putting bottle and all into his mouth and chewing them. As the drugs, a great many of them he thought, began to take their hold on him, he finally had to sit down, for dizziness swamped him. As things blurred and faded in and out, Master thought perhaps this had been a mistake.

~~~

Rick sat on the chair and waited for Nate to wake up. He'd been meaning to talk to the man for several days now...well, he'd really been putting it off. Not that he was afraid of the shifter; no, he just didn't want to get into a fight with him. And Rick was sure this was going to be epic.

"What the fuck do you want?" Rick smiled at the man's tone. "Go away. Don't you think I have enough shit to deal with without you in here trying to drink from me? If I thought it would kill me, then I would let you. But we both know that it won't."

"You certainly do whine a great deal." Nate rolled to his back and Rick, using very little of his own magic, lifted him from the bed and smashed him hard against the wall three times before he smiled again. "Now, this is what we're going to do. You are going to listen to me, then if I think you might have an opinion that I want to hear, I will let you speak. Until then, you are silent."

Nate cursed him. A great deal, if the mumbling coming from the magic that held his mouth closed was any indication. But Rick just let him. Struggling against what held him was futile, and Rick let him wear himself out.

"You came here against your will. Well, boo hoo for you. Most of us had a life before this, and yet here we are working to get this place back to where it was before. So what if you had to give up a life that you loved? Who the fuck cares now? You think the malefactors give a shit that you have several golden trophies to tell others what a wonderful person you were?" Rick laughed. "Let me let you in on a secret, big guy. Do you think if you were dead now, any one would care anymore? I know about your friend's wife and kids. Tough break that, but do you think they would have suffered any less at the hands of the malefactors? Doubtful."

Rick snapped his fingers and Nate started cursing aloud. He let him. It was one thing to be pissy with everyone here, but to him, it mattered little. Rick had been around a long time and had heard it all. When he had heard enough, Rick held his hand up to snap his fingers again and Nate shut up.

"Good. Now, I'd like to ask you a few questions. And so you know, I'll know if you lie to me." Nate said nothing. "Won't get you any brownie points with me if you don't speak, ass hole."

"I want you to go away and leave me alone. I didn't ask to be here, and I—" Rick snapped his fingers and cut him off. When he waited a full minute and snapped them again, Nate started speaking again. "I'm not going to go out on any fucking missions or whatever the fuck you're calling them. I just don't give a flying—"

Rick cut him off again and sat there for several minutes, trying his best to get his own temper under control before he spoke. He supposed that if Remy or the others knew what he was doing he'd be in trouble, but things had taken a turn, and Nate was going to help out or Rick was going to remove his head.

"On the day that you were kidnapped by Benton, did you know that we had all decided to come for you? Not just Remy, but all of us. And it was hard to get Hector to stay behind, too. Goes to show you that no one cares for the way you're treating them, but they didn't want you there, in the hands of Benton, either. You are part of his family, Remy told us, and the fact that he and Skylar were beat up pretty badly saving your ass mattered little to him. Getting you home was all of our priority, and look how you repay us."

Nate said nothing, not even a mumble of a word. He captured the man's eyes and used some of his compulsion to get the answers he was sure that he'd never get otherwise. "Why are you really not helping us?"

"I don't fucking know how to fight." Nate had struggled hard against admitting that, but Rick asked him if he thought any of them did. "I've seen you. Even though you think I'm stuck here all the time, I do get out and about."

"You mean when you went out and got yourself caught." Nate only glared at him. "What were you doing there? Didn't you know that it would be dangerous?"

"I did. But I thought that if I could do this one thing on my own that you'd all leave me to my peace. I didn't know that that thing was coming out the other side until he had me. All I wanted to do was make it so you would leave me alone once and for all." Rick didn't move. He'd not used compulsion on the man. What he was saying now, he was admitting on his own. "There's something else too. Something that I think I got when that drug was put in my body. I have these tats all over me, like you guys I guess, but I also have this thing that I can read. I can...according to this part of my tat, I can command computers."

"What do you mean, command computers? I would guess that anyone could if they have a working knowledge. But to command them? I don't think I understand what you're talking about." Nate asked to be freed and he'd show him. "All right, but you fuck up and I will hit you so hard back there that you'll feel it for months."

Nate said that he understood and moved to the room's computer. There was a television in this room, as well as a house phone. The addition of those, only used within the boundaries of the house proper, had been a startling revelation to them all. As far as they knew, there wasn't a phone company involved. Yet they would ring when necessary, and it would be as clear as if the person was standing in the room with them.

Nate put his hand on the blank screen. Rick moved closer to watch, but far enough back that if this was a trick, he'd be able to defend himself. As the screen started to light up, Nate turned to him, his hand still on the computer as it flickered under it.

"Ask me something that I wouldn't know. About you. Ask me a question about you that no one, not anyone, might know about you." He asked him a question and Nate turned back to the computer to touch it again. "All right. How old is Rick Harmon?"

"It's not...my real name is Richard James. I go down the alphabet...never mind. I change my last name every ten years. I'm really Richard James." Nate asked the computer again. The screen lit up, but not with a green screen as he'd expected, but with a light show that outdid most of the Independence Day celebrations he'd seen. Then Nate stepped back...staggered back, really.

"You were born January thirteenth in twelve seventy two." That was right, and before he could ask him how he'd done that, Nate continued. "You are a pureblood, not made, and your parents both met the sun when you were several hundred years old. They'd had enough, and you mourn their loss daily. You lost your mate...she was murdered when it was discovered that there were vampires in the house. That is why you don't live with a nest of them. It's safer. You have always felt that they betrayed you, and you set about ending their lives when you were able to get out again. You were hurt badly, bad enough that you had to go to ground to heal for several years."

"And how did you get that from the computer? There are no records of my birth. My parents were gone long before the invention of the Internet or any phone service." Nate moved back to the chair this time and not the bed. He told him he had no idea. "But you just came up with information that no one knew and got it from there."

"I also know that our mates are coming, what they look like, and what they are. Your mate is —" Rick told him that he didn't want to know. "But you should. She's not human, as you might have guessed, but she's old, older even than you. And she's already marked up. And pissed off."

"And she's not even met my charming self." He was joking, but Nate said nothing. "And what of your mate? What sort of being is she, and what powers do you suppose she'll bring with her when you fuck her?"

"Benton kills her." Rick started to tell him that wasn't possible, but he continued before he could. "I have these nightmares. A great many of them, but about this woman...I see her clearly now. Her face...I've read poems about beauty such as this. She is simply the most beautiful creature I have ever met. But when she comes to me, just coming to the edge of the property line, he's there suddenly. When I first came here she was just a dream of a woman. I didn't know her or what she might mean to me, but since this happened to me, this drug was given to me by that man, things are clearer, sharper than they were before. Her name is Ila. And she's dead just as we meet."

"At the border." Nate nodded. "And Benton does it. He kills her. In this dream of yours, he kills your other half. Do we all just stand there and let it happen, or is there something else going on at the same time?"

"Yes. To all of that, but I don't know what. It's not clear to me for some reason." Rick told him that it was only a dream. "I told you, I can see her. I know what she looks like and that she's powerful. What do you mean, it's only a fucking dream?"

"A dream, not reality. You said yourself that it's changed. Is it the same every time you dream it? Does he kill her in the same spot? Tear her in half the same way? Are there any differences?" Nate said he didn't know. "Well, when you dream it again, upon waking, write down the details. Remember everything you can about it and keep track. I mean, I have no idea, but if things change, even a little, that means the outcome can as well."

Nate only sat there. Rick wondered what was going on in his head, and when he turned to him, his face full of hurt and pain, Rick was sure that he didn't want to know.

"Why are you being nice to me?" Rick asked him what he meant. "You're all nice to me. Even though I've pretty much shit on each of you, everyone has been nothing but nice. Some of you have been a little tense at times, but no one has hit me."

"Do you want me to hit you?" Nate said no, and that wasn't the point. "Then what is? You think because you act like someone shit on your oatmeal that we should all continue to shit on you? I don't work that way. And the only reason I'm here today is because Remy and a few others have been going out on your shift while you sit in here with your blankie and your thumb up your butt. Get up off your ass and start pulling your own weight, or let me do us all a favor and remove your head. Because from where I'm sitting, that's about all you're good for right now."

"Okay, I amend that last statement. Most of you have been nice to me." Rick just stared at him. "I really have no idea what I'm doing here. I have no talent whatsoever. I don't know how to use the weapons on my body, and other than the computer thing, I don't have anything to add to this team. The first time I go out I get captured, and all of you have to come and rescue my ass or I'd be nothing but fodder on another realm that we can no longer access."

Instead of answering him, or even commenting, Rick stood up, drew his sword, and swung it at Nate. He was aiming for his neck, but before the blade was there, Nate had his own blade out, knocking Rick's away, and was slicing his blade at Rick's neck too, only a great deal closer than Rick cared to think about. Rick let his sword go back to his body and turned to the door.

"You know as much as the rest of us. You're on call at six in the morning. I suggest that you get your body in gear along with the rest of us. We're not going to be carrying your lazy ass again." Nate was standing there still, his sword out, when Rick turned back to him. "Well?"

"I don't like you."

Rick just laughed and moved out of the door. When the door was closed behind him, he leaned against the wall and let out a long breath. He didn't need to breathe, but right now he needed something to calm his frayed nerves. He looked down the hall a short distance when Remy said his name.

"You could have been killed. What point were you trying to make that nearly got your head removed, or do you even know?" Rick nodded. The blade had come very close to removing his head just then, and he didn't think he could answer him without sobbing about how stupid he'd been. "Was it worth it?"

Rick thought about it, really thought about what he'd just done. Was it? Was it worth the idea of being dead now?

"I think so, yes." Remy said nothing. "He'll be put in the rotation now. And with me if you don't mind."

"You two have made friends now?" Rick told Remy that Nate probably hated him more than he did himself. "Then I do not understand why you want to be paired up with him. Are you not afraid that he'll not have your back?"

"He will. He won't want anyone killing me." Remy asked him why. "Because he wants to save that pleasure for himself. And by the way, he has a power now you should talk to him about. I don't understand it, but he has one hell of a power because of the drugs he was given."

Remy said that he would and Rick moved down the hall to his own room. He was inside, his door closed and locked, when he stripped off his shirt and looked down at the tat that had appeared on his belly that morning. He spoke to it now, asking it what he already knew the answer to.

"You belong to her, I'm thinking. Don't you?" The tat, a circle of glyphics that he couldn't read, had started at five last night, just as he was in the yard with the pups. As soon as they started, he looked around for his mate, knowing that it was inevitable that she was coming now. All that he could see were small children that had been there for some time and nothing more. But the burning hadn't left him until he'd had the overwhelming urge to go and talk to Nate.

"Now what the fuck do I do?" There was no answer, not that he had expected one, and he'd done as he needed. But as for this woman? Rick was almost as afraid of her as he was Nate a few minutes ago.

Chapter 12

"There was someone here. I don't think they wanted anything but the drugs, and didn't even bother taking the food with them." No shit, Chris wanted to say, but didn't. Remy was upset enough as it was. "Do you suppose we should put a guard on the place? Maybe a camera?"

"I think whoever it was, they got what they wanted." All the drugs, as Remy had said, and even some of the over the counter stuff was missing. "We can put a guard on it if you want, but I think that would be closing the barn up after the horse has run."

Remy nodded. Chris knew that the man was distracted, but said nothing more about it until he spoke again. He and Remy had been on a drive around to see if anyone needed anything, and they'd come upon the damaged big pharmacy. They had not thought of it before now, having the doctor and all the meds they needed at the compound.

It had been five days since Benton left them. Five days of relative quiet. A few outbreaks, mostly just small things that one person could handle, but nothing major. There were no more large gatherings of malefactors, nor did it seem that Benton was making any more. But they all knew that as soon as they let down their guard, he would come at them. Remy was making them work out every day, in the event that something did happen. It was sort of scary, Chris thought, having things seem...well, so normal. Chris knew that that, more than anything, was what was making Remy so tense.

"The grocery stores are all in good shape. We have started charging for the food now, as you suggested. I think having people work off what they buy for now is going to make them feel better about what's going on around here too. Plus, the cleanup is going much better with the help." Chris had only suggested that they make a work detail from some of the people they were helping to get to the removal of not just the trash, but cars that had been abandoned. And telling them where they came across a body. Remy continued before he could point this out to him. "I have seen an improvement in tempers as well. With them working, they have less time to pick at one another and us."

"Idle hands and all that. My mom used to say that to me all the time when I'd get into trouble." Remy nodded as he started picking up a makeup display and putting it to rights. "Wanna tell me what is really bothering you? It can't just be the fact that this place is destroyed."

Remy moved to the door and looked out. There wasn't much out there. It was daylight, yes, but people for the most part didn't roam the sidewalks just yet. And if they did venture out, it was to get what they wanted or needed and return home.

"The people want to see a funny movie. I was thinking about asking you what one they would enjoy." Chris gave him the title of his favorite movie. "I think you'd be better off telling Skylar. She's seen a few more than I have."

Two weeks ago they had opened the drive in. It had been closed up long before the people started being taken. The weed removal alone had taken the better part of a week. Then there was trying to figure out how to run movies from the ancient projector to the big screen. Finally, they just used some of their magic to do it. The projector looked as if it was showing the movies, in the event someone came into the little room to ask something, but for the most part, they'd been running movies nightly with their magic. It was simpler.

Chris moved to where he was standing and looked out. Remy stood staring at the large wall of bricks before he spoke.

"The other towns…the ones not affect by all this. Do you suppose we will be able to integrate ourselves into their world without questions? I have…over the centuries, I have had to work hard at not being singled out because of my age." Chris started to ask him why he wanted to, but he realized something. Remy was afraid, as they all were. Not of being hurt, though he supposed that was part of it, but of not being accepted. "I know that we have sent out a few others to see what they can find out. A few have returned saying that things are too much for them. The noises alone are enough, one said, to make him have a headache for a week. I don't know if we can keep us beyond the realm of the others when this is finished."

Not if this finishes, but when. It was a good sign, Chris thought, that their leader was thinking positively. But to answer his question? Chris didn't have an answer for him. Wasn't even sure why they were thinking along those lines just yet.

Benton was still out there. At least, they were pretty sure he was. There were still malefactors around; not nearly as many, but enough that it was still unsafe to be out and about unless in large groups. With Dolin and Ward confirmed dead, it did ease the mind, but they still had a long way to go before they were safe. Anyone could be helping Benton, and if they were, then they'd be in deep shit again if they didn't stay on top of their game.

"Before I answer you, why do you ask? I mean, really, we're pretty much self-sufficient here. We have plenty of food. A doctor, hospital, and school. There isn't any mail or Internet, which I find kind of peaceful. We have money to use should we want to, a leader in you, and a jail system in place now. We even have homes that are, in my opinion, nicer than I think some of these people had before. Roomier for sure, and up on the latest of gadgets." Remy nodded and waited for something, but Chris wasn't sure what. "Are you asking me if I want to leave here?"

"Nay, I only ask what you think we'll be doing when this is done. Will we be here for the rest of the earth's days?"

Good point. They would still be warriors with these pretty amazing powers. And thanks to a quick visit to one of the outlying cities, they knew that no human could see them as they did each other. A few shifters did. Vampires for sure, but they only treated them as strangers and not weird ones. The tats, it seemed, were for them to use and see, and not others.

"I think, once this is finished, we will want to take our time in moving out. I'm in no hurry really. I love it here, as I said…it's quiet. But will I want to go away later, become a part of whatever is out there? I have no idea. I guess, like you, we'll have to think about that." Remy asked him if he'd thought about things like jobs and children. "Yes to both. I was an entertainer before this. I don't know why I won't be after if I've a mind to. Kate was a teacher for a time, a doctor when she was younger, and any number of things in between. So she would be able to find work should she need it, if she wants to. But according to Hector, we will be paid forever because of the magic in the other realm. You have always been a warrior. Perhaps you can open your own muscle firm; you know, hunt down the bad guys and bring them in for justice."

"I have been told by Skylar that I would be very good at that. Only I cannot be the judge on what their payment is. She said that I would only be the...what you called it, muscle, not the one that passes their sentences." Chris laughed and nodded. "Skylar wishes to have children and open a restaurant. She said that before this, as you have said, she was good at something and would like to do it again."

"We're immortals. I'm pretty sure that even if we don't know how to do something, we have plenty of time to learn it." Remy nodded, and Chris had a feeling that whatever was on his mind, this was only a part of it. "Kate and I want to have children as well. But I think we're going to look into taking on some of the ones that have been left behind from this."

"The other world, it's gone. So many people have lost everything. Not just lives, though that is enough, but homes, photos, as well as memories that can never be replaced." Ah, so that was the unspoken problem, Chris thought. He was thinking of what had been destroyed in the name of greed. "All those people that have died over there have been left where they lay. At least the ones here have a place to call home. Dead or living. They have nothing left of their own; all their memories and things have been left in a place that no one will be able to return to. Not from this realm, I'm told."

"They have called this their home, Remy. And from talking to a few of them, they have it much better than they did in their realm. I think, for the most part, they're happier too." Chris watched as a woman moved along the streets, her cart in front of her and a gun slung over her back. Her eyes darted everywhere as she moved. When she saw them, she waved but never stopped moving. "People will soon feel safe here too, I believe. Once Benton is dead and all the malefactors with him."

Remy said nothing but watched the woman as he did. When another person came out of a house a few doors down from the woman, they both watched as they huddled together with their guns and carts and made their way to the other street, where the grocery store was. He wondered if they had planned this, or if the second woman just happened to be watching for anyone to come by so as not to be alone.

"I wish to ask you something." Chris told him that he could have anything he wanted. "I should like for you to wait first before answering. I want you to do me a favor and move to the other town. The one where there are people."

"Move out." Remy only nodded, then looked at him. "Are you asking me to move out for a reason? Because if I've done something wrong, I would hope that you'd let me know."

"No. Nothing like that at all. I should like for you to purchase a home in a neighborhood. Live among them for us. Find out what we have missed, as in news reels. I understand that we might not be up to the latest news on things, and it would seem horribly remiss of us if we were to suddenly appear in a town and not know current events. Come here, when you can and it is safe, and give us information. A learning class on what we should know." Chris was surprised at the request as well as the reason behind it. "When I was alone, just working the task as it came, it wasn't necessary for me to know much of anything that was going on. Not the newest fashion, should I have cared, or who was running for an office. What the price of eggs were. But with this many people, we will seem out of place if we don't even know the most basic of current events. Don't you agree?"

"I do. I can gather newspapers for us to read. Magazines, as well as some other means of information. Perhaps I can even figure out a way to make the projector work here and bring in current movies too." He'd meant it as a joke, but Remy said that sounded like a great idea as well. "May I ask why you picked me?"

"Davis was my first choice, as a matter of fact. But I dismissed him because of his hardened ways. As a cop, he would be more inclined to gather the current events that pertain to laws and regulations. What crimes are being committed and the punishment of them. You are more...current in a great many things. And more open minded as well. I'm not saying that we don't need to know laws and regulations, but I think we'll need a more broadened gathering of facts." Remy laughed before he spoke again. "Davis would not have thought of movies and magazines. He would have brought us police reports and graphs and line charts. He is a good man, but he is very jaded, I think."

Remy seemed more relaxed after Chris agreed he and Kate would do it. He'd have to talk to her, but he didn't think she'd mind. And he started a mental list of things that he might want to bring back that they were lacking in as well. He wondered how hard it would be to bring out a few computers and get them hooked up.

~~~

"She's coming." Rick nodded at his friend, and then asked her who. He'd been meeting Janell here for several months now, if for no other reason than to just catch up on some of his other issues. Mostly his home and other properties. "The woman I told you about before. You have to watch your back with her. She's not really...I was going to say she's like you, but that would be an understatement. She's meaner."

"I'm not mean." Janell snorted at him. "I'm not. I'm right all the time, and I get upset when others don't see my way. I need a sign that says that to them before they open their mouths to disagree with me. Don't you think?"

"You're mean. But she's still coming. And when she gets here, you won't be able to come to see me again." He asked her why. "Because, my dear friend, she's your mate."

"I don't think so." But the conversation he'd had with Nate came back to him. "She's really coming here? I mean, soon?"

"Time doesn't mean much to me, and you know that. But I would say about a fortnight." Two weeks. He had two weeks of being free left. "She will bring with her a great deal of baggage."

"What sort of baggage?" Janell told him what she knew. "So this woman, who is meaner than me, is coming here with her entourage? Why do you think she needs four others with her to come here?"

"Don't know, don't care. All I know is that she's making plans. And she's closing up her house too. I don't think the two of you will suit, but it's not my business." Rick nodded. He didn't think they'd suit either. He was as set in his ways as most people his age were. "When she gets here—and like I said, it will be soon—I'd like to be warned about it. I don't want to be hanging with you and lose my head because she's a jealous bitch."

"You don't like her." Janell snorted again. "What is it about her that has you hating her so much? I mean, you get along with everyone, but this woman has you pissy. Why?"

"You don't know, do you?" Rick asked her what she meant. "You know her too, or at least you know of her. She's Lucia. Lucia Alvarez."

Rick nearly fell back, he was so shocked. "Lucia is dead. She was killed when the war broke out, and was caught on the battlefields killing the dying for a meal. The council said that they'd taken care of her, and that I had no worries that she'd find me."

"You really are out of the loop, aren't you? She was found not guilty. Not that I know who did it, but she had proof that she wasn't the one doing it." Rick held onto his fear like it was a coat and it was blowing in a heavy storm. "She's sworn on her life that she was going to find out who turned her in for this. I'm guessing that she can hold a grudge like you can. Are you all right?"

"I have to go." He nodded and moved back into the shadows, and had nearly left the area when Janell called him back. "I really need to get back to the encampment. I have...I'm on call."

"Yeah, well, okay, but here is the paperwork you asked me to bring and the rest of the things you asked for." Rick took the satchel and turned away. He was nearly ready to transport himself to his room when Janell called him back.

Turning, he looked at her. "Want me to tell you when I hear anything about her?"

"Yes. Please. I'd like to know everything you know. You know how to contact me." She said that she did. "All right then. I really must go."

He was standing in his room seconds later. Dropping the satchel on the bed that he'd never slept in, he sat down on the big chair that faced his window. None of the rooms really had a view, but right now he didn't even care.

Lucia Alvarez. She was coming here. And when she.... Rick got up to pace. Christ, he was going to be in a world of hurt when she figured out he'd been the one that had turned her in that day all those decades ago. And the worse part of it was, he knew that she had a temper like no one he'd ever met.

He'd been at war. Not just with those that he was fighting against, but with himself too. His mate, Angelica, had died, and he'd been hoping for a way to end his life that did not make him suffer. He'd been selfish even then, he knew that, but he had just wanted his life to end. An easy way out.

Rick had been gifted, he supposed that was as good a term as any, with the ability to stay in the sunlight. Nate had been right in saying that he was born a vampire and not turned into one. But what he'd not say, and might not have known, was that he came from a very long and very strong line of vampires. One of the first families, his mother had always told him. And with that long line had come powers that newer vampires might not ever obtain.

He'd been on the battlefield, not unlike the one that Remy had described when he spoke of Hector coming to him. Bodies were thick in the grass, their blood forever staining the soil beneath it. Swords and knives, or most anything, had been used to fight. He'd had a sword of his own, having gotten it from his father the day he'd decided that ending his life was better than living without his mate. As had Remy, Rick had been ready to die, his body beaten, stabbed, ready to fall down and become ash, when he saw her.

Lucia was not a nice person, which he supposed was a massive understatement. Or so he'd always heard about her. Her way to end an argument or even a conversation that wasn't going her way was to kill. Most of the time by snapping the other person's neck—though that did not limit her killing ability—and walking over them as they lay there.

But she'd been there, walking among the dead, lifting them up and feeding upon their bodies before dropping them where they lay and moving on. It had been the way that they'd done things for generations, he supposed, but...Lucia wasn't a vampire.

Lucia was a faerie. Not just a normal faerie, but one that commanded armies when needed. Lucia was a faerie of war. The worst kind of magical creature, as far as he knew.

War was a fact of life, he knew this better than most. War faeries were known to simply show up on a battlefield and turn the tide of a fight in any direction that they wanted. It mattered little to them who benefited the most, or what the war was really about. If they wanted a certain side to win, then they did, simply because they wanted it that way.

They could not be bought. There wasn't enough money in the world to sway them to either side. Promises meant nothing to them. They had everything that they ever wanted or needed. They took no sides but their own. It was said that if they were in the middle of the field fighting for one side, it would be nothing for them to turn their backs on them to suddenly begin fighting for the other group. Rick had seen it happen once in his lifetime.

But Lucia was on the field then, killing the dying and taking from them as if she had been a victor in all this. When she lifted a large man up, drinking from his throat, Rick saw her face. It was a face that he knew that he'd never forget so long as he lived.

Rick moved to the window and watched as several of the children collected leaves. It was fall now, the time of great color and cooler nights. When one of the puppies moved by a pile of leaves that had been raked up, scattering them to the four winds, he smiled. The dogs had been a great distraction and joy to have here. Then his thoughts turned to Lucia again.

Getting up again had been a chore that afternoon. He'd not wanted to live, not to move off the field where he'd be nothing in a few hours anyway. But Rick knew that he had to tell someone, let them know that this woman was going to get caught, giving all magical creatures a bad name. He'd been so young, he thought now. Stupid and young to think that he could make any kind of difference in what others did.

"I tried. Stupidly, but I did try."

His voice sounded harsh in the nearly empty room. Unlike the others that lived here, he'd not wanted anything in this place but a few pictures, which he'd brought from his home, and his books. Rick was an avid reader. He had books about the very battleground that he'd been on that day. He looked at it now, remembering the words that had been said to him.

The council, when he was able to see them, had told him that they'd had reports before about a woman doing this. His mother and father had sat next to him, one on either side, when he was able to get into the large castle to plead his case. When they showed him a picture of the woman he described, they nodded and conferred for several minutes before speaking to him again.

"Lucia Alvarez will be brought before this council and her head removed." He started to ask if there would be a trial, but his mom put her hand on his as the head councilman continued. "It has been brought to our attention before that she has been making herself known to humans, without thought of the consequences that it might have to the rest of us. There will be a reckoning with her; she will be made an example of for those who would dare try this again. Thank you, young Richard James."

Three months later he'd been given word that Lucia had paid the price for what she'd been doing and that he was safe now. His parents had been so happy…he had been too. After being cooped up in the house for all that time, Rick had gone out and never returned. That had been over seven hundred years ago. And now here she was coming back to get him.

"And she's my fucking mate."

Before You Go...

HELP AN AUTHOR

write a review

THANK YOU!

Share your voice and help guide other readers to these wonderful books. Even if it's only a line or two your reviews help readers discover the author's books so they can continue creating stories that you'll love. Login to your favorite retailer and leave a review. Thank you.

AWARD WINNING, BESTSELLING AUTHOR

Kathi Barton, author of the bestselling series Force of Nature, lives in Nashport, Ohio with her husband Paul. In addition to writing full time Kathi likes to spend time with her eight grandkids, three children and three children-in-laws. She writes to relax and have fun.

Her muse, a cross between Jimmy Stewart and Hugh Jackman brings them to life for her readers in a way that has them coming back time and again for more. Her favorite genre is paranormal romance with a great deal of spice. You can visit Kathi on line and drop her an email if you'd like. She loves hearing from her fans. aaronskiss@gmail.com.

Follow Kathi on her blog:
http://kathisbartonauthor.blogspot.com/

www.ingramcontent.com/pod-product-compliance
Lightning Source LLC
Chambersburg PA
CBHW032132170626
46808CB00006B/2198